Ask Me Again

Ask Me Again

Florida Ann Town

Copyright © 2017 by Florida Ann Town.

ISBN: Softcover   978-1-5434-2092-0
       eBook   978-1-5434-2093-7

All rights reserved. No part of this book may be reproduced or transmitted in any form or by any means, electronic or mechanical, including photocopying, recording, or by any information storage and retrieval system, without permission in writing from the copyright owner.

This is a work of fiction. Names, characters, places and incidents either are the product of the author's imagination or are used fictitiously, and any resemblance to any actual persons, living or dead, events, or locales is entirely coincidental.

Any people depicted in stock imagery provided by Thinkstock are models, and such images are being used for illustrative purposes only.
Certain stock imagery © Thinkstock.

Print information available on the last page.

Rev. date: 07/25/2017

To order additional copies of this book, contact:
Xlibris
1-888-795-4274
www.Xlibris.com
Orders@Xlibris.com
761721

CHAPTER ONE

I CAN'T EVEN breathe. Words build inside my head, piling on top of each other, cramming into the corners of my mind until I can't hold them in any longer and they spew out in a hot, angry stream that almost burns my lips.

"What the fuck are you thinking?"

"Shhh!"

Shhh? She's shushing me? Telling me to be quiet?

"Sahira, are you crazy? Don't you even care? This is your whole fucking *life* you're throwing away."

Her fingers trace a pattern that I can't see, scrolling against the bedspread. Like everything in the room, it's richly coloured and softly luxurious. She watches her fingers like she's never seen them before, then clasps her hands together, lacing the fingers together before stretching them out, touching the tips of her thumbs to each other. It's like she's playing some kind of game, and the outcome will determine what she's going to do – whether she'll answer my question, or continue to ignore it. When she finally speaks, her voice is soft.

"My mother doesn't like that word."

"What?"

"That 'f' word. She doesn't like it when girls say that."

The air drains out of me. I can't believe what I'm hearing. Sahira's whole life is about to be wrecked, her future trashed, all our plans destroyed, and she's fussing about a word her mother doesn't like to hear. I don't even know if there's any point in saying anything after that. It's like she's talking in her sleep or something. She's saying words, but they aren't making any sense. Does she even know what she sounds like? Does she even believe what she's saying? Or care?

"Earth to Sahira. Come in."

I wait for her smile, for the response that has always been there. But this time, there's nothing. "Sahira, are you even listening to me?"

She looks at me. Her eyes are beautiful – large, dark and expressive. Her eyebrows float above them, almost joining in the middle. Her skin is a pale tan colour – in the summer I get browner than she does. Probably because I spend more time in the sun. Like many Indo-Canadian girls, she likes to protect her skin, covering up, sitting in the shade. Maybe that's why she looks like she should be on the cover of a magazine, and I look like I should be somewhere in the back pages, where they advertise freckle cream, running shoes and stuff to do outdoors.

"Yes," she says. The word floats out on the smallest of breaths, like it's escaping from a very deep and dark place. "Yes." There's another pause. "I'm listening. But it doesn't matter. Don't you see?" Her hands stretch forward in supplication. Her fingers are long and slender, with shapely nails. I look at them, picturing them in the exaggerated poses of Bollywood dances. I glance at my own hands, knotted into fists, with nails chewed down to the nubs, and shove them in my pockets.

"Don't you see?" she repeats. "There's nothing I can do about it." She looks at me, than repeats, almost to herself. "There's nothing I can do about it. I don't have a choice."

She isn't talking about the "f" word anymore. It's back to our original discussion. I close my eyes for a minute and take a deep breath. I'm trying not to shout, trying to speak rationally, trying to make her see how utterly ridiculous this is. She won't listen to me, but I'm trying to get her to listen to herself.

"Sahira – you do have a choice. You don't have to marry someone you've never met, just because your father tells you to."

"But I do," she says. No infliction. No raised voice. Nothing. Just unquestioning acceptance. "That's how my mother and father got married. Her parents met with his parents and they arranged it all."

"That's something that happens in the old country," I say. I'm still trying to be rational – trying to make a logical point. "This isn't India. This isn't the Punjab. This is Canada. And you're a Canadian."

"No," she says, "You're wrong. I am Canadian, but I'm Punjabi too. And in the Punjab, when your father arranges a marriage, you don't question it. You simply do it."

There's a long pause before she continues. "That's the way it's always been." Another pause. "After all, who knows better than he, what is best for me?"

She raises her eyes and looks at me for a moment, as though she's somehow clinched the argument, then drops her gaze back to her folded hands. She massages one thumb with the other, her fingers skimming over each other like leaves blowing in the wind. As though some uncontrollable force has taken over and she'd just a robot, moving to directions I can't hear.

"But you've never even met the guy." I repeat.

There's a long pause before she answers. "That's true, but he's my father's cousin. So my father knows him."

"How can your father know him – when's the last time your father was in India?"

"He doesn't know him personally, but he knows the family. This is his cousin," she repeats, as though that explains everything.

I shake my head.

"I don't get it. It just doesn't make sense, Sahira. Do you really believe a seventeen-year old girl can marry a 45-year old man she's never even met? I don't understand how you can think it's a normal thing to do. You don't know anything about him. You don't know what he likes, or doesn't like. What does he eat for breakfast? What kind of music does he like? What's his idea of something that's fun to do?"

She continues to play with her fingers. I know she can hear me, but she isn't paying attention to anything I've said. It's like she's slipped into another dimension.

"Come on, Sahira – face it. You don't have anything in common. You don't have any of the same friends, or interests - I don't see how you can hope to make a marriage work when there's absolutely nothing to base it on, except that your father wants you to marry the guy."

There's a long pause before she answers. "My mother didn't give my father any sons." The words flow so smoothly, so matter-of-factly it sounds as though someone has poured them into her head and she only has to open her mouth to let them slip out. I can't accept that she really believes what she's saying. "Now my father needs someone to help with the business. When I marry his cousin, he can come to this country and help my father."

"So why can't you help your dad? You're an intelligent woman. This isn't the Dark Ages, for god's sake. Women even have the vote now. Did anyone tell your dad about that? You're graduating from high school – graduating with honours. Doesn't that tell him that you're intelligent enough to help out in his business? You've got more education than he had – and he managed to be successful. Why does he think you're not just as capable?" It's all I can do to restrain myself from grabbing her shoulders and giving her a good shaking.

There's the smallest exhalation of breath, as though she's gone over this many times and has to force herself to repeat it. If she has said it, it's something she's only whispered to herself. She's never told me about not being able to work for her father, or having to import a cousin from the Punjab.

"My father needs him. He's chosen him to be next in line."

I try to wrap my mind around that. Next in line for what? Inheriting the family fortune? Inheriting the business? This isn't the Royal Family, determining who will be next to sit on the throne. I don't know what she's talking about? I take a deep breath and try again.

"So what kind of experience does he have? What does he do in India that's so great?"

"I don't know."

I roll my eyes. "Great. No experience, never met him – I'm sure he's going to fit right in with the family and the business."

She looks at me and the silence ripens between us, like something that will splatter if I poke at it. Maybe I can offer an alternate plan. Maybe not - but it's worth a try.

"Okay, then let his cousin immigrate. That's what people do when they want to come to this country. That's what your father did."

She shakes her head. A small, sad movement, like she's feeling sorry for me because I can't seem to understand what is so clear to her.

"What about veterinary college?" I continue. "What about that? You've dreamed about being a veterinarian for as long as I can remember. Doesn't that count for anything? Are you just going to throw that away?"

"My father would never let me do that – you know that. That's why I didn't tell him about the applications I sent off."

This is the first I've heard about *that*. For years now, she's talked about wanting to be a veterinarian. I've helped her, as we sweated over the applications and dreamed about how things would be, while we thumbed through the stacks of college and university catalogues in the school library. We went through them, one after another, looking for the perfect school. One that offered credentials that would lead to acceptance in veterinary medicine. One that offered scholarships. One that would let us both escape, because the plan was for us to live together and share an apartment. She'd go to school, I'd write my book. It was going to be a dream come true for both of us. I remembered some of the other things we'd talked about when we were making our plans.

"We can even get a car." That was one of the things I'd said. It had always been my dream. I'd been driving ever since the day I was legal – Dad insisted on it. He said every girl should know how to drive, and he made sure I took a good driver instruction course, but that was just the beginning. After I finished the course – and passed with flying colours - he spent hours with me in the car, letting me drive, pointing out everything that I overlooked. Encouraging me to be proactive, to watch for other drivers and not to count on them to do what they were supposed to do. And to look out for pedestrians, for people on bikes, for dogs running loose – a whole bunch of stuff. When he finally said I was ready to drive on my own, I felt like I was probably the best qualified driver in the whole country. Getting my own car was the crucial step to fulfilling my dream. I always assumed that we would both drive it, because there were so many places I wanted to go, and it would be easier if we could both drive, but whenever I mentioned it, Sahira gave a thumbs down, or changed the subject, or just ignored my comments.

"Why not?" I'd asked. "We'll need a car and it only makes sense for both of us to drive it."

"You can get one if you want, but I won't drive it. I'd be terrified. Just the idea of it scares me silly."

She had to be kidding. I started to laugh: "Come on. There's nothing to it."

She shook her head. "Maybe for you, but not for me. Just the idea gives me the shakes."

That was the first time I've heard about that – but no big deal. If she doesn't want to drive, she doesn't have to. "Fair enough. I'll drive, you navigate."

We talked of many things as I helped her with those scholarship applications, but marriage was never one of them. I remember one of the problems that popped up on one of the many forms we filled out.

"I have to tell them about my community service and volunteer work and all that – you'll have to write that for me," she'd said, laughing. "I can't write about myself."

"Sure you can. Don't be so modest."

"I'm not being modest. I just can't talk about myself. It feels like bragging."

I couldn't change her mind, so I did write the community service section. I put down all the details about the 'Stepping Out' program she started at the Terry Fox library – an after-school program for a group of grade five girls that met every Tuesday afternoon. She'd been doing it for three years and the girls loved it. She let them choose a topic, something they were interested in, then challenged them to read about it in the library, then go exploring to find out more.

They went on all sorts of adventures. One of them, I wished I could have joined in: a geology hunt along the river bank to find different kinds of stones, then matching them with pictures in their text books, or library books, identifying each stone and trying to figure out how it got there and how far it might have travelled. They looked at the way water affected the stones, pointing out erosion patterns in the rocks and in the surrounding areas. One water adventure flowed into another. They learned about Port Coquitlam's water system – where the water came from, how it was treated and purified, and how it got into everyone's home. They toured the dykes, checking the heights of the river against the official flow gauges. That led to mapping expeditions, mapping each of the blocks they lived in, adding in the library, the school, the shopping centre, creating maps of their own neighbourhoods – the list went on and on.

Sahira laughed when she read it. "That's very nice – you make it sound very interesting – but it's not really important. I mean, that isn't the kind of stuff they care about. It was just a bunch of girls having fun and doing stuff together."

"You're wrong, Sahira. That's exactly what selection committees gobble up."

She turned serious then. "That would be nice if it were true, but I think they need something more important than that. Just working with girls isn't much."

I should have seen the warning signs then, but I didn't. I missed it entirely – *just working with girls* made it sound like something that wasn't very worthwhile. And there were other signs I missed out on as well. She'd always known her father wouldn't pay for her to go to university, but I thought I'd managed to convince her that if she won a scholarship, she wouldn't have to ask her father for money, so he'd have no reason to keep her at home. That was the big issue. Or at least, that's how it seemed to me. It all seemed so simple then.

Now, watching her as she calmly accepts her father's edict, I realize it was nothing but a game she was playing. She wasn't really trying to fool me, as much as convince herself of something that she knew would never happen. In some other universe, she would like to become a veterinarian – just as, when I'm in wishful thinking mode, I would like to become a ballerina. But it isn't something that's going to happen in this lifetime. Not for me and, it seems, not for her either. She can't say 'no' to her father and my stocky legs would never fit under a tutu. Plus it would take two of those gorgeous guys in white tights to hoist me up in the air. So – two dreams land in the trash.

We've shared so many dreams over the years, but not being together had never entered my mind. Letting go was too painful. Somehow, I tell myself, I have to convince her that there is another way out. That there is a viable option. Something her father would have to agree to. And something that she would have to believe in, enough to fight for.

"But if you got accepted…" She cuts me off with a quick wave of her hand.

"It was just a dream – and some dreams simply don't come true."

She reaches behind her and takes something from under her pillow. "This came yesterday," she says, handing me a large, brown kraft-paper envelope. "Go ahead. Look at it."

I ease open the flap and reach inside. There's a booklet, and a sheaf of papers. I glance at the top page and do a double take.

"Oh my god! You did it! You got the scholarship."

Sahira nods. A faint smile touches her lips before it disappears.

"Yes. It's quite a good one. $25,000 each year, for four years." She pauses. "It would have been wonderful."

"Would have been? You aren't going to go?" I hear the words, but my mind can't take in what she's saying. "That's enough to pay your whole tuition and living expenses. That's your degree! The whole thing! Now you don't have to ask your father for a penny. He can't say no to this."

She shakes her head. "You still don't understand. My father doesn't believe girls should do things like that. He would never permit me to become a veterinarian. Even with the scholarship. As far as he's concerned, my job is to be a wife to whomever he picks, and to give him grandchildren."

"Sahira – listen to what you're saying. You can't believe that. You're more than just a – a baby machine."

She doesn't respond.

I hand the envelope back to her.

"I better go."

She continues to sit, silently, on the edge of the bed. Finally her hand reaches out and she touches the envelope. She puts it beside her and uses her finger to trace invisible words on it. After a minute, she picks it up again and hands it back to me.

"Here. Please take it. I don't want my father to see it. You can throw it away for me."

I pick up the envelope and walk out, shaking my head. This is crazy. On the way out, I see her mother, standing in the kitchen, as always, busy cooking something or other. I used to love coming into Sahira's kitchen. Her mom let us sample stuff, and sometimes she let us help her. I didn't know half of the stuff that she used in cooking – just that the spices smelled wonderful and made everything come alive. It was a big change from what we ate at home. Most of dad's live-ins seemed to think take-out covered the basic food groups. And that I should be grateful if they made me a peanut butter or a jam sandwich for my school lunch – a sandwich that was always soggy by noon. I quickly learned it was better to make my own lunch, and after a while, I even started to try making dinner. That's when Dad joined in. He'd barbecue the meat while I did the veggies or the salad or whatever. It wasn't fancy, but it was better than the steady diet of pizza or buckets of stuff from the Colonel.

Sahira's mom looks up, smiles, and I smile back at her. I guess she didn't hear me say 'fuck' or she wouldn't be smiling. Or maybe she did, and just doesn't care, as long as it isn't her daughter who's using the word.

CHAPTER TWO

SOMETIMES I WISH I could be like Christy. She's such a cool person, in so many ways. Mostly because of the way she acts. She always seems to know what she wants, and then finds a way to do it. My life is bounded by my dad's dictates. He's the one who has to approve everything I do, everything I want, everything I buy. Mom isn't much help. I think she'd like to be, but she doesn't know how.

As far as I can remember, they've never had an argument. At least, not that I've ever heard. That doesn't mean she always agrees with him. She doesn't – and I can always tell when she's mad about something by the way she works in the kitchen, slamming things around, banging cupboard doors and all that. Not when he can hear her, of course. Mostly she's really quiet, but when she gets mad, the volume goes up. 'Way up. And I know he hits her sometimes. He hits me too. He's got a really bad temper and when someone or something gets him riled up, he gets physical. Sometimes I'm scared of him. I mean, the way he looks at me sometimes, like he even hates me. And I don't know why.

Mom told me once that he really wanted his first born to be a boy, and when I came along he was pretty disappointed. And I guess he was even more disappointed when it turned out I was going to be his only child and he'd never have a son. Mom told me she'd miscarried a couple of times after I was born. She never went into much detail, like she never said if the babies were boys or girls – or maybe it was too early to tell - but lately I started thinking about it, and wondered if he was responsible for them. I mean, if he'd hit her or something, could that cause a miscarriage? It wasn't something I could ask her about. We never really talked about anything personal and private. Sure, she told me about the birds and the bees and all that, but nothing on a personal level.

Now that I think about it, she's never even said much about what it was like when she was a kid. I know she grew up in the Punjab, just like my dad did, but other than that, I really don't know much about what their lives were like. I've never met any of my relatives – they all still live back there, and dad says it costs too much to fly there, so my aunts and uncles are just names on a sheet of paper. Sometimes I wonder if I have any cousins – I'm sure I do – but I don't know what they might be like, or even what their names are. And I wouldn't know them if I ran into them on the street. I always thought that someday I could go to visit them. That's one of the dreams on my bucket list. I mean, family should count for something, shouldn't it?

Christy doesn't have an extended family – there's just her and her dad, and now there's a step-mom and a step-sister, but Karli's still just little, so she isn't like a real sister. I mean, you can't talk to a four-year old about anything serious. And I know Christy doesn't get along with her step-mom. I sometimes wonder if there are any step-moms and step-kids who *do* get along with each other. You sure don't hear about them if there are.

Christy was real mixed up when her dad decided to re-marry. I know she really missed her mom, and her dad had a string of girl-friends after she died, before he hooked up with Tiffany, but I think Christy was happier with the girl-friends. They didn't hang around too long. But it looks like Tiffany is there to stay.

Anyway, that's not my problem. Christy's right. I don't want to marry someone I've never met. I always imagined there would be some kind of courtship. That's an old-fashioned word, but I don't know a better one to use. Like when you date someone – only it's deeper than dating. Not that I'd know – my dad has never let me go out on a date with a guy. I can only go out with another girl, or with a group of girls. He'd freak out if he knew that sometimes the gang I went out with had guys in it. But you never really get close to a guy that way. Maybe I've seen too many movies, but I always thought before you got married, you went out with a guy, got to know him, got to decide if you really loved him or not. And then you could have sex if you wanted to. If you were responsible about it. And then maybe you got married if things worked out okay.

Now *that's* something I'd never be able to talk about with my parents, much less do. In their books, you don't have anything to do with a guy until after you're married. Just like things were a couple of centuries ago. My parents don't seem to realize these are modern times, and people do have sex before they get married. But the way things are going, I'm not even going to get kissed before I get married, much less have sex. I can't even imagine what my dad would be like if I came home pregnant. Not that there's any chance of that, but still, I can't help but think that it would serve him right.

Sometimes I wonder what this guy I'm going to marry, is going to be like. He's one of my dad's cousins, so I guess he'll be something like my dad. I mean, look something like him. Or maybe not. But I sure hope he doesn't have my dad's temper. I don't think I could live with that. Not like my mom does.

Mom tries to be kind and to make up for dad being so miserable. Even if she can't talk about it, she does nice things for me. Like buying me clothes. Well, that's not really a good example, because my dad has to approve of them. Anything that he thinks isn't modest enough gets sent back. Maybe a better example is my bedroom. Mom's decorated it to death, but as far as I'm concerned, it's nothing but a beautiful prison. I'd be happy to strip the walls and clear the room out so there wouldn't be anything left in here but a bed and a desk. I wouldn't even need a bed. Just a mattress on the floor – if only I could be free to come and go like Christy does, but that's pure wishful thinking.

I'd like to tell my dad I'm not going to marry his cousin, but I hate to think what he'd do to my mom if I did. I've heard him sometimes, when I've done something that he thinks is wrong. Sometimes he'll slap me, but mostly, he takes it out on my mom.

"What kind of daughter have you raised?" is how he usually starts out. Then he makes her life hell for a few days. Won't talk to her. Just stomps around the house and glares at her, and finds fault with everything she does. Pokes at the food on his plate but won't eat it. Tosses shirts on the floor because they aren't ironed properly. Chucks his shoes into the back room because they aren't polished properly. That's when the violence happens. It always seems after one of these sessions, the only thing that clears the air is if he slaps her around. I've heard her crying when she's in her room, but she's never cried in front of me, so I can't say anything to her. We both just pretend everything is okay.

Sometimes I'm just sick of all the pretending that goes on in our house and I wish I could just walk away from it all. But I know I can't.

There's a soft knock on my door. That will be my mom. If it was dad, he'd just bust into the room without knocking or anything. Wouldn't matter if I was stark naked, he'd just shove his way in.

I open the door, and mom's standing there with a tray in her hands.

"I brought you some dinner," she whispers, edging her way into the room and depositing the tray on my desk. "Your dad is a little upset, so I thought it would be better if I just brought your dinner so you could eat here, instead of coming downstairs."

"Are you okay?" She's looking red around the eyes, like she's maybe been crying.,

"I'm fine. It's just … well, you know how your dad gets sometimes. So I thought this might be easier."

"Thanks mom." I give her a gentle hug, but she winces and pulls away.

"I, um, hurt my arm earlier. Silly me. I went to get something out of the cupboard and it fell down on my arm."

We both know that's not true, and it confirms my suspicion that dad's hit her again for some imagined infraction. Why does she put up with it? There must be something she can do besides just be a doormat to a cranky old man.

"Can I help?"

She shakes her head. "No, but thank you for asking. I'll be okay." She pulls the fronts of her long-sleeved cardigan more tightly around her. "I'll just have to learn to be more careful." She turns and slips out the door, closing it softly behind her, so quietly that you can't even hear the closing 'click'.

I look at the door for a long time before I turn to the tray on my desk, but I'm not hungry. All I can see is my mom's red eyes, and the way she cringed when I touched her arm. If I had a gun I'd shoot that stupid old man. But I wouldn't kill him. I'd rather see him suffer, like he's made my mom suffer.

CHAPTER THREE

WALKING HOME, I still can't believe what's just happened. This morning, today seemed so ordinary – just a day like any other day. When I got Sahira's message earlier I thought it was just another text. Like we text back and forth a dozen times a day. Silly things. Funny things. Like reaching out and giving a hug to a friend. Certainly nothing important. So I answered her, like I usually do:

> Hi gf. Wuzzup?
> Gotta CU
> When?
> Now
> Ur hse?
> Pls

I'd left my room and gone downstairs, where Tiffany was engaged in her favourite activity: watching TV. Soaps, talk shows, anything at all that was just fluff and gossip and didn't require thinking. I've never seen her with a book, or anything that required any effort. Just an endless diet of TV and National Enquirers. God, what a mess her brain must be.

"Sahira asked me to come over. I think she needs help with her homework."

Tiffany's lips quirk into a semi-smile. "Sahira needs help, or you do?"

Way to go Tiffany. Get a dig in, any way you can. God, I hate that woman. Really, truly hate her. But I have to be polite or my dad gets on my case. Like she's never in the wrong and it's always me. Always my fault. I don't think he even listens to me anymore. I don't think *anybody* listens to me anymore. Except Sahira and Anton. I pause in the doorway.

"I've already finished my homework."

She glances at her watch. "Don't be long. I've got things to do today. You're sure you're not going out to see Anton?"

I don't even both to answer that one. She behaves as though Anton is some raging sex maniac that I'm hanging out with. She doesn't even know him, never even met him for god's sake, but she still puts him down. Or maybe she just dislikes him because he's not white. I don't know how she found out he's Korean, but somehow she did. Maybe a school picture or something. Whatever. But there's no way I'm going to tell her she doesn't have to worry about the sex stuff, because Anton plays for the other team. It's a private little joke, and I laugh to myself every time she makes another one of her stupid comments. I can't decide if she's more racist or more homophobic – whatever, she's sure got a twisted mind. Anton's been a good friend for years and years. Not being stereotypic or anything, but it's like he's one of the girls, and takes Sahira's place when she can't go somewhere with me – which seems to be most of the time.

Sahira's parents won't let her go out by herself. "Nice girls don't go out unless they're with a family member," her dad says. According to Sahira, his philosophy is that girls are only allowed to be on their own if they are going to school, because the teachers are supervising them there. Outside of that, they go with their family to the Gurdwar for religious and other events. They help their mothers to shop and cook and look after the house, so when they are married, they know what to do.

Sahira doesn't have any brothers or sisters. Her aunts and uncles are all back in India so there aren't any cousins to hang out with and her dad is usually too busy to go anywhere. Her mom doesn't go out unless he's with her – I guess she's under the same restrictions as Sahira. The bottom line is, my friend hardly gets to go anywhere. When we were little, she lived right next door, and she was allowed to play in our yard. Then they moved, and now everything is different. She's not allowed to go to the movies with me, or to hang out at the mall with me, and even coming to my house is a major event, so most times I just go to her house because it's easier. Sometimes I pick up a movie and we watch it at her place. Or we just talk.

Anyway, when I want to go do something and Sahira isn't available, I call on Anton and he's happy to go. Not just to the artsy stuff that people think is all that gay guys like – but to all sorts of things from skate boarding to volunteering for Rivers Day cleanups. He's just fun to be with, and given the mess that my dad has made of relationships and marriages, I'm not anxious to link up with anyone anytime soon. Anton is comfortable to be with, and that's good enough for me.

Today, when I got to Sahira's house, she was waiting at the door and almost dragged me up the stairs into her room.

Her bedroom is like no other I've ever seen – except maybe in magazines. It vibrates with colour. Three of the walls are deep rose, the other is a brilliant orange. That sounds crazy, but it works. The windows are swathed in curtains – layers of curtains, in saffron and gold. The walls are decorated with glittering pictures. It feels like something out of a movie set – vibrant, exotic and exciting.

It's a pretty dramatic contrast to my bedroom -- four walls painted pale blue, venetian blinds with no curtains, and no posters or other decorations. Just a plain, bare room. I like it that way. It's sort of a reflection of me – just plain and ordinary; nothing fancy. No one has ever said I was pretty. I'm not fat, but people have called me stocky. Or sturdy. Whatever. They never say I look like a model, because the only thing I could model would be rugby shorts or hiking boots. And that's what my bedroom is like. Plain, functional, no ruffles or flounces and totally unlike the rest of our house. Tiffany has everything but my room so decorated up that it looks like a box of chocolates. There's stuff everywhere and layers of decorative pillows on almost every chair, sofa, footstool, recliner or whatever. I won't even describe the other bedrooms in the house – you'd have to spend at least five minutes every night removing pillows before you could get into bed. Tacky. Totally tacky. But what can you expect from someone named Tiffany. What a stupid name. Tacky Tiffany. I can't for the life of me figure out what my dad sees in her. When he first brought her home, it seemed like she was just another one in the parade of girlfriends he'd had since my mom died. Well, there was his second wife, but that never worked out. Either for my dad or for me. I guess not for her, either. She left when I was seven, and, except for the girlfriends who drifted in and out, it's been just me and dad ever since, that is, until Tiffany came into the picture. Somehow, she had staying power where the others didn't. Well, that and the fact that she was pregnant. She's managed to make my life hell for the past four years and from where I sit, it doesn't look like my dad's been having all that much fun either. The only good thing that came out of it was my little 'sister'. I can't believe my dad is her father. I don't know if dad believes it either, but he always refers to her as his daughter. She doesn't look like him at all. But she's a girl, so I guess it's natural that she looks more like her mom.

Anyway, once I got to Sahira's room, she closed the door, leaned against it and took a deep breath.

"Sit down," she said, waving me to a brocade-upholstered chair. "You aren't going to believe what's happened."

I grinned at her. "Believe what, girl friend? What are you up to now?"

"I'm getting married."

"You're what?"

"Getting married."

It took me a minute to wrap my mind around that. She isn't allowed to date, never goes out with a guy – so how come she's going to get married?

"To who?"

"You don't know him. I haven't met him yet either. My dad just told me. It's one of his cousins in India. In the Punjab."

"But – you can't marry someone you don't even know."

Sahira didn't even blink. "Yeah, I can."

"But …" What can I say? The whole thing just didn't make sense. I reached out to her.

"Don't," she said. "Don't hug me. I'll cry if you do."

Well, if a hug was going to start her crying, that meant she wasn't as stoic as she was pretending to be, and deep down, she really does care. I can respect that.

"When is this going to happen?"

"Soon," she replied, then gave a smirky little laugh. "My father is being real generous. He says I can finish school – he'll let me go to grad, and after that we leave for India. Like almost the next day. That's where the wedding's going to be – in his hometown in the Punjab - so I can't even ask you to be there for the wedding." She paused. "I guess I'd always thought you would be my bridesmaid, and I would be yours, when the time came."

The room filled up with silence. What could I say? I was glad the wedding wasn't going to be here. I didn't think I could handle it.

"How about the prom?" I asked.

She shook her head. "No. I can go to the grad ceremony, but not the prom."

"But you've already got your dress."

She laughed. It wasn't a funny laugh. "That's what I thought too. Mom talked me into getting a traditional Punjabi outfit - *shalwar kameez* – because grad is such a special occasion. I should have known better." She grimaced and bit her bottom lip, like she's trying hard not to cry. "I thought it was so lovely. The dress, I mean."

"It was. I mean, it is. That colour is spectacular on you. Hardly anybody can wear a deep red like that, but it's just so you -- and the embroidery is to die for."

"Yeah. To die for. Well, mom and dad must have been planning this for quite some time, because it turns out that what I thought was going to be my prom dress is actually my wedding dress."

I never thought about it before. Sahira doesn't wear traditional Punjabi clothing. At least, I've never seen her wearing it. She doesn't wear it for any special occasions that I know of, and she certainly doesn't wear it at school. She just wears the same as everyone else wears. Well, almost what everyone else wears. Now that I think of it, she doesn't wear short shorts or cut offs, and doesn't wear cropped tops or anything that's in any way revealing. And she wears long sleeves a lot – even in the summer. A couple of times, when we were changing for gym or something, she had some awful bruises. To hear her tell it, she's a super klutz. Always bumping into something or falling down the stairs or running into a door. But the truth is, she's one of the most graceful people I've ever known. Maybe I should have paid more attention to those bruises.

I can't believe how blind I've been all these years. How could I not have noticed?

Thoughts bounce around in my brain, like mini-tornados, whirling up stuff from all over the place. Things I hadn't paid attention to before. Suddenly, those bruises don't seem so innocent now. She hasn't been bumping into things or falling down the stairs. I've never even seen her stumble. It looks more like someone has been beating on her. And there's a limited number of someones in her house that you could point to. But – would her dad really do that? The thought scares me, but I guess it's possible. You never know what goes on in someone else's life. Just thinking about it gives me the heebie-jeebies. But what scares me even more are some of the things I've read in the paper, or seen on TV recently. Things people have said about what happens to some young South Asian girls when they are married off to strangers. Or even worse, what happens when they marry someone their parents don't approve of. And suddenly I'm scared for Sahira.

Sahira's dad is awfully strict with her. Strict to the point of being cruel. She might have a beautiful room – but I'm suddenly thinking it's more like a beautiful prison. And then I start thinking about her mom. Her mousy little mom, who never raises her voice. I'm willing to bet she gets bullied, too. And maybe even worse. If Sahira has bruises, I'll bet her mom does too.

When I look back, it seems she never does anything but spend time in the kitchen chopping up stuff and cooking stuff. I mean, it's like every time I go there, she's always in the kitchen. Sahira said she was preparing stuff for the Langar – a sort of free kitchen that they have in their Gurdwara. I don't really know how to explain what that is. It isn't a church, even though that's where they go to worship, but there's a lot more happening, according to Sahira. She's invited me to go with her a couple of times, and I did. It was really interesting. Everyone has to cover their heads. They have headscarves to loan you if you don't have one of your own, and lots of men who visit tie something that looks like a handkerchief around their head. Everyone takes off their shoes before they go in and the whole atmosphere is – I want to say warm but that's only part of it. Friendly, helpful. Even though I was a stranger they made me feel welcome. When she invited me to go with her the first time, Sahira said if I want to be a writer, I should experience as many different things as I can, and she was right. It wasn't at all like I thought it would be. Then I laugh. I can't really see Tiffany doing anything like that – but I'll bet my dad would. He'd love it. He's always up for any kind of adventure.

Sometimes I think about my mom and wonder what she would have been like. I was so young when she died – I don't really have any clear memories of her, but Dad has shown me pictures. And talked about the things they used to do together – and the things that she used to do herself.

"She was a pretty independent cookie," he said. "She'd try anything." He paused for a minute, as if he was remembering some of the things he did. He must have told me a thousand times that I look just like her and a lot of times, that I act like her.

Sahira's mom is a whole different matter. I sometimes wonder about her. Doesn't she ever do anything just for fun? She doesn't go shopping without her husband, not even to buy a dress for herself. She can't go to the library by herself. I'll bet she's never set foot in a Starbucks. What sort of life is that? And is that what lies ahead for Sahira?

No. That can't happen. My friend is too intelligent – too nice for that kind of a life. There has to be another way.

Things keep roiling around in my head – but I can't see a way out for Sahira. Unless. Unless – it's a crazy thought, but what if she ran away? Left home? Just escaped? How could she do it so her parents wouldn't know where she was? Because if they could bring her back, I could really see her dad getting super mad – and even getting violent.

Maybe that scholarship really could be her escape route? How would that work?

I mull on it, all the way home. It could be done, I think. Her folks don't know she's won it, so if she just disappeared, they wouldn't know where to start looking. But I'd have to tell my dad about it. Or would I? Thompson Rivers University is in Kamloops, so I'd have to find a way to justify going there. I don't have a scholarship – haven't applied for anything, and haven't a chance of getting one in any case because I'm not brilliant like Sahira. I'm an okay student, but she has something extra that I just don't have. So, if not a scholarship or award of some sort, what will my excuse be? There has to be something else – something that will seem logical. Something that my dad will agree to. Tiffany can be counted on to screw up anything I want to do. Her plans for me seem for me to be a permanent baby sitter for Karli. That's the little girl that she had shortly after she and my dad got married. Well, whether Tiffany likes it or not, me as a live-in baby-sitter isn't going to happen. That's something she'll just have to get over. Either that or find another baby-sitter. Or maybe even start looking after her own kid, for a change.

But how about Sahira's marriage? Can Sahira's dad actually make her get married? That's something I have to find out about too. I know her dad has dual citizenship but I don't know if Sahira has. And maybe in India, he can make her get married, whether she wants to or not. I'm going to have to find out a lot more information before I make my move – but somebody has to do something and it looks like I'm the only candidate.

When it comes to marriage and divorces and relationships and all that stuff, my dad should be an expert. He's screwed up enough times that he should at least know what not to do. I'll talk to him about Sahira's marriage – without telling him who it is, so he won't have to hide anything once she escapes. And somewhere along the way, I have to figure out an excuse for me to go to Kamloops.

That's when I remember something that was on TV a little while ago. Some brainiac was explaining that he invented whatever it was that made him a .com millionaire before he was old enough to vote. He said he would never have thought about it if he'd just gone lock-step from high school to university, like most of his buds did. Instead, he took a gap year. A year out, to travel, think, decide on his future and all that stuff. I like that idea.

I'll tell my dad I want to take a gap year, before I go to college or whatever. We've never really talked about what I'll do after I graduate. I'm not really university material – but college? That might be more believable. He'll laugh, and Tiffany will shit bricks, because that might mean spending a whole bunch of money on me. She'd rather spend it on herself or on Karli. She grumbles about everything I buy – and that's pretty darn little, when you get right down to it.

Or maybe I could convince my dad that I'll get a job of some kind. He's bound to be enthusiastic about that, but he'll want to know what kind of job I'm getting, and Tiffany will point out that I'm not qualified to do anything but baby sitting. And that's not a full time career.

I'm starting to get mad at Tiffany already – I mean, really pissed off, because I can just see her messing up my plans. I'll have to talk to my dad privately. Without her big ears hanging out. Before she gets a chance to screw things up.

I really do need to find a job of some kind. And then I get a brilliant idea. There's been a huge pine beetle outbreak in the Interior over the past few years, and forestry companies are hiring lots of people to plant trees. It's summer work, not a permanent job, so I could do that and maybe make enough to live on for the rest of the year, if Sahira and I shared a place. It can't be that expensive to live in Kamloops.

Yeah. I like that idea. That gives me an excuse to leave home and do something that's even ecologically beneficial. Maybe if I stress that part of it, I won't have to even mention Sahira. I'll be independent, earning my own money, so Tiffany can't squawk about it. The more I think about it, the better I like it.

By the time I get home, I'm almost ready to start packing and I can hardly wait for Dad to get home, so I can tell him about it.

CHAPTER FOUR

THAT NIGHT, AFTER the news hour is finished, I decide it's time to talk to my dad.

"If you know something really, really wrong is going to happen, but it isn't illegal or anything, would you do anything about it?" I ask.

Tiffany laughs. "If it isn't illegal or anything, there can't be much wrong with it."

"Please. I was talking to my dad."

"Well ex-cuse me." She picks up a magazine and starts thumbing through it.

"Christine, that was pretty rude," Dad says.

"I'm sorry," I mutter. "But dad – I really do need to talk to you about something. In private. Please."

There's a long pause before he responds.

"All right."

Tiffany riffles the pages of her magazine, clearly annoyed, as he leads the way out of the living room and settles himself at the kitchen table. I sit opposite him, trying to figure out how to begin.

"Now, what's this all about?" he asks.

"Can I tell you without telling you who it is?"

"Give it a try."

"Okay. Well, what if someone had to get married, but they were still a minor. Could someone make them do it?"

"Oh, come on now," he laughs. "Don't tell me you're pregnant."

"No!" I jump up from the table. Oh, shit! How can he jump to a conclusion like that? Now I'm really pissed off. I want to have a serious discussion and he starts off totally on the wrong foot. That's the kind of remark I'd expect Tiffany to make, but not my dad. I guess my frustration is showing, because he stretches out his arm and gives me a hug.

"Hey, I'm sorry. Bad joke. Come on – sit down. I was just kidding. Honest."

I sit down again, but he's got me so riled up it's hard to put words in the right order.

"So what's the problem?" he asks.

I try again. "What if a girl doesn't want to get married but her father says she has to?"

He shakes his head. "If she doesn't want to get married, she just doesn't. That's it."

"For sure?"

"No one can make anyone do *anything* if they don't want to."

"Not ever? I mean, maybe not here, but maybe somewhere else?"

"Christie, you're either going to have to tell me a lot more about what's going on, or give up. I can't give a sensible answer with the information you've given me." He pauses and looks at me. One of those looks that parents use when they know you're hiding something. The look that goes right through you. "Or rather, with the information you haven't given me. I think there's a lot more to this than you're telling me."

I think hard about what to say next. He's right, of course. "It isn't that easy. I, like, promised not to tell."

"Okay, you've kept your promise. You asked my advice? Here it is. If you don't want to do something, no one can make you. And if you don't want to get married, you don't have to. This isn't the Dark Ages."

I can almost hear his mind whirling around, trying to figure out who and what I'm talking about before he continues. "Christie, I honestly don't understand what you're getting at. But if something wrong is going to happen and you can stop it, then anybody with an ounce of decency would do so."

"Okay. That's what I thought." I stand up and put my hand on his shoulder – then drop a kiss on the top of his head. "Thanks, Dad."

I'm hardly out of the room before Tiffany's out in the kitchen, quizzing him.

"What was all that about?"

"You know, I'm really not sure. She wouldn't give me any details. She's worried about something – but I can't figure it out."

Tiffany dismisses it. "Probably just something that happened at school. She'll get over it."

"I don't know. It's not like Christie to go off on a tangent. She's a pretty level headed kid."

Tiffany opens the fridge door. "Want anything to drink?"

"What? Oh. No – no thanks."

The fridge door thumps shut, a pop can fizzes open, and Tiffany's footsteps trace her progress back into the front room.

Great. I was afraid Tiffany would figure it out. As much as I dislike her, I have to admit she's got a pretty good brain when she wants to use it. At least, it's pretty good when it comes to sniffing out gossip and scandal. But Dad's given me the okay to try and remedy a bad situation and that's enough for me. I don't want either of them to figure out who's involved in this – not until I've decided what to do. Right now, I'm drawing a big zero when it comes to inspiration, but there has to be *something* I can do to help Sahira.

There's no way I can disrupt the wedding – it's going to be in India, so that's completely out of the question. What I have to do is figure out an alternate plan for Sahira – something that will take her completely away without leaving any clues behind. If I can do that, none of this has to happen. I think I know what to do, but I need to bounce my idea off of someone else – someone who can poke holes in it, and help me make it foolproof. I can't involve my dad in this, and I'd never talk to Tiffany. They'd both be shocked. Not just shocked, but dead against it. At least, I think they would be. Even given what dad said, I don't think he'd approve of what I'm thinking. But there is someone I trust – and who might be willing to help.

I call Anton. He can't believe it when I outline the situation. He likes Sahira – she's a good friend – and the idea of throwing her life away like that really rankles.

"So what are you going to do?" he asks.

"I'm going to write to the university, and accept that scholarship for Sahira."

There's a long silence before he answers. "Can you do that?"

"I think so."

There's another pause while he mulls that over.

"Then what?"

"I won't be going to university, but maybe I could get a job in Kamloops, so me and Sahira can move in together. I don't want a year-round job, but I thought if I could be a tree planter, I could make enough to pay my bills for a year. Then I could start on my book."

"Will your dad let you do that?"

"Hey – we're adults now, remember? Well, close enough that it doesn't matter, so we can do what we want. Anyway, I thought I'd tell him I was going to do a gap year, before I made up my mind about what I wanted to do for real. I mean, I know I want to be a writer, but most grownups just laugh when you say that. I could take writing courses, maybe, or something like that, but I don't really want to spend more time in school and anyway, I don't think taking courses would really do much good. Or impress anyone. Especially my dad. So I'll have to put some other idea up front, and that one is just wild enough that it might work."

"Hey, that's cool. I might do something like that too. Things have been getting pretty shitty around here."

I know what he means. He's tried a couple of times to come out to his parents, but they aren't paying any attention. Or they won't believe him. Or maybe they just don't want to believe him. It doesn't seem to matter what he says, they have their own ideas about him. I guess a lot of parents are like that when they only have one kid. That's something Anton and I share – we're both only children. Well, I am except for Karli and she doesn't really count. She's a whole lot younger than I am, and she's a step-sister in any case.

I know my dad just has a fuzzy sort of notion about what I'm going to do after I leave school – something that doesn't call for much talent, or training. Probably work in an office or something until I get married. Jeez! What kind of future is that? But Anton's parents think he's going to be a brilliant scientist. It doesn't matter that he isn't the least bit interested in science. The funny part is, he could be anything he wanted to be, because he really is smart. He and Sahira would make a good pair. Now that I think of it, Sahira's an only child too. That makes us almost like the Three Mousketeers. I have to smile when I think of that. While dad was going through his endless stream of girlfriends, he seemed to think watching reruns on the TV was an acceptable form of child care, so he plunked me in front of the TV to watch hours and hours of old Disney programs. There was other stuff too, that the experts on child care probably wouldn't have approved of, but I found them interesting, even if I didn't always understand them.

"We'll talk tomorrow," Anton says.

"Okay," I agree, and we hang up.

I take out the letter from TRU and look at it again. There's a form for Sahira to fill out, accepting the scholarship and registering at the university. There's a time limit on it so I figure the best thing to do is to fill it out for her and discuss it later, when I've had a chance to convince her that this is for her own good.

Sahira's signature looks like it should be easy to copy – but it isn't. Her writing is straight up and down – no fancy curlicues; no slant to the right or left, very even, very precise, and except for the capital letters, each letter is exactly the same height as the one before it. It almost looks like a computer-generated signature or some kind of calligraphy, but I know it's not because I have several samples of her writing in front of me.

My first try is pretty awful. I guess I don't have a knack for forgery. Lucky this is a once-only event. At least, I hope it is. I try again. My own writing slants to the right and my letters are raggedy. I guess that says a lot about her and about me, too. Maybe the people who say they can read fortunes or know stuff about you, just by looking at your handwriting, aren't so crazy after all. About ten tries later, I sit back and look critically at my latest effort. It looks pretty good. I do one more, just to make sure, then turn to the letter I've printed out from my computer – the one to Thompson River University, accepting, with thanks, their scholarship offer – and sign Sahira's name to it. I fill out the registration form using block letters, because that's easier than trying to write everything, and put Sahira's signature at the bottom.

There's a niggling little voice in the back of my head that's pretty shocked by what I'm doing. Yes, I know it's forgery, but I tell myself it's for her own good. I'm even beginning to believe myself.

I compare the signatures one last time, fold the letter and slip it into an envelope. I can mail it tomorrow, on the way to school.

The next morning, Anton's waiting for me at the end of the block. "Did you do it?"

"Yep." I wave the envelope in front of him. "All ready to go."

He gives me a high five. "This is so cool! I can't believe you're actually doing this."

I grin. "Someone has to. She won't do it for herself."

"Okay. I spent some time on the computer last night and got an address you'll need to visit, before you sign up for a tree planting job. It's all about training, companies, pay, gear you need to have – like boots. You can't wear your ruby red slippers." He grins, then pauses. "Only thing is, they say that if you want to get a tree planting job, you should apply in January or February. I know it's April, but I hope it won't be too late. There were a couple of crews still advertising for planters, so maybe there are a few vacancies left. Tree planting is such a great cover story – your parents will never guess what's going on. And it really does pay well. You'll have enough to live on for the whole year. Easy. That'll give you lots of time to write a best seller."

Anton's the only one who hasn't laughed at my dream of becoming a writer.

"Are you thinking about coming too or were you just blowing hot air?"

He gives me a long look. "Yeah. I really am. It's sounding better and better all the time."

We walk the next block in silence, then step up to the mail box. Anton makes a ceremony out of holding up the flap so I can drop the letter in. He's such a goof. I laugh a lot when I'm with him.

"That's it," I say, lifting the envelope up to the box. "Her fate is sealed."

But before I can slip the envelope in the slot, he closes the flap.

"I just thought of something," he says.

"I did too. I can't mail this until you take your hand off the flap."

"No. Just listen for a minute." He takes my hand – and the envelope – and turns me away from the mailbox. "First thing is, you don't have a return address for her, do you?"

"What do you mean?"

"I mean, when Thompson River sends anything to her, they're going to send it to her parents' address, right? And then they'll know exactly where Sahira is."

"Oh, please. I'm not that dumb. I gave General Delivery, Kamloops, as her return address."

"Okay. But I've got a better idea. I've got a friend in Kamloops – maybe we could use his address for a letter drop? That would look better than General Delivery. And it would be more secure."

Aha! Now it's 'we'. Anton's with me. Great. I tuck the letter back in my back pack and we carry on walking to school. That's when he proves himself to be better than a friend. He's a miracle-worker. Before first period is over, he texts me that his friend says we're welcome to use his address. My plan is working out perfectly! Sometimes it's hard not to feel smug, but this is really going to be great.

I'm smiling to myself, and flicking my thumbs over my phone when a voice cuts into my thoughts.

"Christine, turn off your cell. You know the rules," Mr. Robertson says. "You keep it turned off or I confiscate it."

"Whoops, sorry," I mumble.

He's just standing there, looking at me. I raise my phone, to show that it's off, but he shakes his head.

"I asked you a question."

"Sorry," I say. "I didn't hear you."

Someone in the back row starts to laugh.

"I'm aware of that," he says, ignoring the laughter. "Let's try again."

So now I'm back in the regular routine. Bo-ring. Anyway, I answer his question and he goes on to nab someone else while I scribble answers in my book. I glance at my cell. I've turned off the ringer, but that doesn't mean I can't text, as soon as he's out of the way. It's like a game in class – everyone has their head down, but they aren't looking at their books, they're texting, under their desks.

That night, I re-do Sahira's letter of acceptance, with the address Anton's given me. I think about adding a line, saying that I now live in Kamloops, but decide against it. It's probably better to just leave it as it is. I text Anton, thanking him for his help, and I'm surprised by his return message.

"CU in Kam plntg trees."

"Rlly?"

"Yep."

So – now I'll have my two best friends with me in Kamloops. I'm not sure what's happened at his house. I can guess, but it doesn't really matter anymore. It's just going to be a bonus having him there. If everything works out – and there's no reason to suppose it won't, Sahira will get her degree and become a vet, I'll make enough money to support myself while I start my writing career, and my two best friends will share the adventure. Life couldn't be better.

CHAPTER FIVE

IT'S SATURDAY MORNING – one of my favourite days of the week. Sunday means the weekend is almost over and Monday is back to school, but Saturday opens a huge window of free time. I'm sitting in my room, doing nothing – breakfast is over, my homework is done for the weekend, and all I have to do now is decide what I want to do today. Suddenly, my phone blinks. It's Sahira. I flick it on.

"Hi gf. Wazzup?"
Cn U cum over?"
"Sure. CU"
"Tiffany, I'm going over to Sahira's," I call, as I walk out the door.
"Oh – I wanted you to look after Karli for a while. I have to go out."
Great. So why didn't she ask me an hour ago. How come she has something to do every time I want to leave the house? It's like I'm some kind of permanent baby-sitter for her kid. Well, technically, I guess Karli is my step-sister, but I never think of her that way. She's just Tiffany's daughter. Besides, step-sister almost always means someone wicked and evil, and Karli isn't that. She's just a little kid. A cute little kid, actually, and the fact that her mother is a pain in the neck isn't her fault. Evil step mother could apply to Tiffany, if she was a little bit brighter and intentionally evil. But she's not. She's just dumb and a pain in the neck.
"Sorry – I'll do it when I get back. I won't be long."

I walk out the door, closing it quietly behind me. Without even looking, I can tell she's standing there looking like a thundercloud, and know that I'll be in deep shit when I get home, but right now I don't care. She can look after her own kid for once.

The sun actually feels warm on my face as I walk to Sahira's house. Mid-April is too early to expect real summertime weather, but sometimes we get lucky and have a preview. Like a little teaser. Then it goes back to normal and everyone feels grumpy again. Today, though, it's a pleasant walk. The ornamental cherry trees are in bloom, shedding blossoms that look like pink snow. Some of the early daffodils in the neighborhood gardens are smiling a cheery greeting and further down the block a couple of guys have their shirts off while they push lawnmowers over the grass. They're smiling, and so am I.

I can't help but wonder what's up with Sahira this time. I hope it isn't another shocker like her getting married.

She's waiting at the door and almost runs me up to her room.

"Look!" she says. "It's a picture of Gurbash."

"Gurbash?"

"The guy I'm going to marry," she says, like I should have known just by looking at him or something. Jeez, she's really getting into this and now I'm beginning to wonder if it's even worth while trying to help her escape. She waves the picture in front of me and waits, expectantly, for a comment.

What's to say? He just looks like an ordinary guy. "Nice," I say.

She holds the picture at arm's length, tilting it this way and that, then brings it up to her cheek nuzzling against it. She's clearly talking herself into something, and I don't know what to say. Then I take another look at the picture.

"I know he's your dad's cousin, but he doesn't look very old." I look at the picture again. "When was that picture taken?"

Her hands drop. "I don't know. I didn't think of that."

"Didn't you say he was around your dad's age? The guy in that picture sure doesn't look as old as your dad."

She looks down at it again, strokes it with a finger, then puts it aside. "Yeah, you're right. I guess I was just being silly. But I thought he looked pretty nice."

"He does," I admit. "Or he did, whenever that picture was taken. But some axe murderers look pretty nice too." If she's already talked herself into this – and decided that it's going to be okay to marry this guy just because doesn't look like a raving maniac – it's going to be even harder to convince her that there's another way out. Harder because now I'll be spoiling something for her. We'll have to talk about this pretty soon, but obviously this is not the time, so I change the subject.

"Hey – guess what I'm going to do this summer?"

She looks up, blankly. "I dunno."

"I'm going to make a whole whack of money over the summer so I can spend the next year writing my book."

That catches her interest. "How can you do that? Won't you be baby-sitting Karli? Or is Tiffany going to pay you to baby-sit?"

"Hah! Like that would ever happen. No – I'm going to get a job as a tree planter. They make fantastic money – the ad said some of them get $15,000 for ten weeks of planting. That would be almost enough to live on for a year."

She considers this. "That could be interesting. But isn't it awfully hard work?"

"What's so hard about digging a hole and putting a little tree into it? I've helped dad in the garden lots of times, and digging holes isn't exactly rocket science."

"Are you sure? There has to be more to it or they wouldn't pay that kind of money."

I nod. "Yeah. Well, maybe because you're outdoors all the time. I mean, like sometimes it rains. Or something."

"Maybe. Where will you go?"

"I'm thinking about Kamloops. They had all that pine beetle kill a few years ago, and some of it's been logged off. They've had a couple of forest fires and things, so I guess there's lots of space that needs to be filled up with trees again, and they're going to need lots of help. I haven't actually applied yet – but that's what I'm thinking about."

"Well, good luck to you. I hope it works out."

On the way home, Anton texts me.

"Got smthn 4 U"

"Wat?"

"U'll C"

"Wen?"

"Now. C U at prk.

The park – it's been one of my favourite places since I was a little kid. Hyde Creek Park is one of those parks that combines nature walks with playing fields and playgrounds for little kids. It's not far from the river – the Traboulay Trail runs close to it, so it's really great for jogging or biking and there's almost always someone out walking a dog. Some parks are so isolated and empty that they're downright scary, but this one isn't like that.

I send an OK back to him, and head home to get my bike. I'm no sooner in the door than Tiffany's on my case.

"I told you I had to go to out. Where were you? You have to look after Karli for me."

Oh, shit. I'd forgotten all about Tiffany and Karli. And where's she going that's such a big deal? I mean, holy crap – how much shopping can one woman do? I shrug. "Okay. I'll take her to the park. She likes that."

"Well make sure you put sunscreen on her. And take some water for her. And don't let her get dirty."

Yada, yada, yada. Like I don't know how to look after the kid when I spend more time with her than Tiffany does.

I nod, then go get Karli ready. It's too far for her to walk, but she can ride the crossbar on my bike. I grab my helmet and pick up Karli's as well.

"Hey, kiddo," I call out. "Wanna go to the park?"

She nods. She's a neat little kid, really. Too bad she has Tiffany for a mother.

"Okay. Do you know where your sunglasses are?"

She nods again. She always knows where her stuff is. It's pretty crazy for a four-year old to be as well organized as she is. She certainly doesn't take after her mother.

"You go get them and I'll get some water for us to take."

"Can I have juice instead?"

"Sure. What kind?"

"Brown juice. With fizzies."

I laugh. "That's not juice. That's pop – and you know it. Shall I ask your mom if you can have some?"

She shakes her head, no. Then I think, what the heck. Why not? What's a can of pop going to do to her? She deserves a treat once in a while. I grab a couple of cans from the fridge, snag a handful of cookies to go along with them and stuff it all in my pack. Then I reach back into the fridge and grab another pop for Anton.

I text to let him know I'm riding over with Karli. I don't ride fast when she's on the crossbar, so it takes about fifteen minutes to get there.

He's waiting, with a big grin on his face and a bunch of papers in his hand. As usual, I get a big hug hello, then he turns to Karli.

He bends down so he's looking her right in the eye. "Wow. You're as pretty as your sister."

Karli looks up at me. Tiffany has told her never to talk to strangers – and Anton's a stranger to her.

"It's okay, Karli," I say. "This is my friend, um, William." Anton's eyebrows fly up and he makes a funny face, then grins. I'll have to explain later, but I know if Tiffany finds out I was with Anton while I was baby-sitting Karli, she'll go berserk. Meanwhile, Anton goes along with the gag.

"Hi," he says, holding out his hand. "What's your name?"

Karli gives his hand a dubious shake but says nothing as she backs away, grabbing me by the knees.

"She's a little shy," I tell Anton. But I'm thinking to myself, he's probably the first Korean person she's ever seen and she doesn't know what to make of him. Oh, well. Sooner or later it's going to hit the fan, but in the meantime, I'll just play it cool.

Anton stands up and brandishes a stack of printouts at me.

"Here's your homework!"

"Homework? For what? I already did all my homework for the weekend."

"This is your homework for the summer," he says. "I printed out my copy and I printed out one for you, too."

I thumb through the pages. "This looks like an exercise program."

"That's exactly what it is."

I look at the first page. It talks about special equipment you need to do the exercises. It's a different kind of workout and it sounds hilarious. It tells me to attach one end of a band to something solid like a doorway, and put the other end onto a handle of some sort, and then practice shoveling.

"This is crazy," I tell him. "I know how to shovel."

"Maybe so – but can you do it all day long? Without hurting yourself?"

"Of course I can."

He shrugs. "I thought we could do some of this together – you need to get in some walking training too."

"Walking? I can walk for hours."

"Up a mountain, with a pack on your back, from sunrise to sunset?"

"Oh, come on," I say. He's making this sound some kind of big deal, when it's just walking around in the woods. I've seen pictures of forests around Kamloops – lots of tall skinny trees and no underbrush. "It's no big deal."

He put on his serious face. "You're wrong, Christie. It is big deal. Planters don't call themselves industrial athletes for nothing. If you want to make money, it's all about how many trees you can plant in a day. That means you work fast and you work hard. You don't get paid so much every week – you get paid for piecework. For the number of trees you plant. So if you want to make big money, you plant lots of trees."

I look at him. "So?"

"Think about it Christie. If you're not in pretty good condition, you won't cut it. So – you need to start training. Me too. Who knows, maybe with a little luck, we'll get sent to the same area."

Karli's looks interested now. "Where are you going, Christie?" she asks. "Can I come too?"

"Oh, nowhere," I say, shaking my head at Anton.

"Yes, you are. He said so," she says.

Great. Now I know she's going to tell Tiffany.

Anton silently mouths a question. *"Have you talked to your dad yet?"*

I shake my head, *"No."*

He nods. Okay – he's got the message. "Hey, look, Karli! There's an empty spot on the round and round. Wanna go ride it with me?" She starts to back away, until he adds,"…and with Christie?"

She looks at me and I force a smile. "Sure. Let's do that. It's one of my favourites."

Sure it is. I love going around in circles and getting falling-down-dizzy. NOT. Oh, well. I guess there's no getting out of it.

CHAPTER SIX

C HRISTIE'S PRETTY SHARP. I thought I could fool her with that picture of Gurbash – make believe I was looking forward to seeing him. But she spotted something that I'd missed. I guess I was looking for a Prince Charming, or for him to turn out to be someone better than my dad. If he's the same age as my dad, this *is* an old picture. A real old picture. I've seen pictures of my dad when he was younger, and we was an okay looking guy. I mean, not movie star handsome or anything, but okay. And Gurbash looks about the same. Or I should say, looked about the same. But if he's old, like my dad, he isn't going to be so sharp.

I wish I could tell from the picture if he's good natured or not. That makes all the difference in the long run. Looks can fade, but a temper is always there.

Then I think about the summer. It's going to be a long summer if Christie's away up in Kamloops. I don't really have any other friends. Sure, I know people at school, but they aren't real close. I couldn't bring them home – I never know what my dad's going to be like. Or my mom. Christie just floats through and ignores them. We're mostly in my room anyway, so she doesn't really spend any time with them. I mean, she says hello when she comes in and goodbye when she leaves, if they happen to be around. But other than that, there's not much going on.

I wonder what tree planting would be like? It sounds like it might be fun, but there must be more to it than it seems, or they wouldn't be paying big bucks for people to come and do it. Not that there's any chance that I could do that. Not go away by myself. Even going with Christie wouldn't matter – he wouldn't be in control of me if I was out in the woods somewhere, and he couldn't handle that. And when he gets upset with me, he always takes it out on my mom. But someday he's going to have to see me go. Someday pretty soon. Once I'm married, he won't be there to boss me around all the time. And then I remember something he said a while ago when he was talking to my mom. He didn't know I could hear him, but I could. And I wasn't sure what he was talking about then.

"There's lots of room in this house for someone else," he told her. "We don't even have to make a suite in the basement."

Mom mumbled something I couldn't hear, and I went back upstairs to my room. I wondered what he was up to now? Maybe he was going to rent out a room to a college student or something, and get a little income from that? He was always fretting about money, so maybe this was another of his schemes. Most of them didn't pan out and this one probably wouldn't either. I put it out of my mind. But now the words came back with grim meaning.

He meant for Gurbash to move in with us. And if that happened, Gurbash would feel indebted to him. Both for giving him a place to live and for making it possible for him to come to Canada.

I grabbed my stomach and thought I was going to be sick.

I'd never get away from him. It didn't matter what kind of person Gurbash was, my father was going to be the head of the household forever. And I'd never be free of him.

There had to be something I could do. Some way to escape. Christie talked me into applying for scholarships. It was all done in secret, and I never thought anything would come of it, but now I've won one. For a few minutes, I thought it was going to be my route to freedom. I could go away to university and he wouldn't be standing there, screaming and shouting at me and my mom. But then, of course, I knew he'd never let me go. That was why all the applications had to be secret. I could see it now for what it was – just a big game like some kind of fairy tale. Instead, I would be chained to this house forever.

Now I wished I'd talked to Christie earlier – told her what things were really like in our house. Told her about how violent my dad was. But that wouldn't have done any good either. There wasn't anything she could do about the situation. There wasn't anything anyone could do.

CHAPTER SEVEN

OUR REC ROOM looks really great. Dad did a lot of work on it – not that he was so keen on it, but Tiffany kept on his case about having a place for Karli to bring her friends. Like what friends? She doesn't play with anyone in our neighbourhood. If Tiff wanted her to play with other kids, she could let her go to kindergarten, but for some weird reason she doesn't want Karli to do that. But she went on and on about 'play dates'. Nag, nag, nag. If I was my dad, I'd lock her in a closet, just to get away from that motor mouth of hers.

After all her nagging, the room got finished, but it almost never gets used so I've sort of taken it over. It's got its own TV, a mini-kitchen, and separate bathroom. The furniture's pretty neat – IKEA stuff, but it looks modern and it's pretty light weight. Easy to move around. I could almost live down here. If I'm lucky, I might find something like this in Kamloops for me to rent.

I spread the TRU stuff out on the desk and look through it. It looks like an interesting place, and has a ton of great programs. The booklet is full of information about the university, student housing, loans, course selection and that sort of stuff. Then I look again at the letter announcing Sahira's scholarship.

I wish I was as smart as Sahira. I'd love to win a big scholarship like this and move somewhere else. It would be like winning the Lotto. But I'm not that smart, so it's never going to happen. Still – some of this stuff looks encouraging.

Like maybe you don't have to be a super brain to get a scholarship. Like, everything isn't rocket science. Like, yeah. Sure. In my dreams.

Then I take a second look. Maybe it isn't impossible. I'll talk to the guidance counselor at school, and see if I might qualify for something.

* * *

"You know you're too late to apply for scholarships for this year," Miss Abel says.

"What would happen if I just wanted to take, like, one course this year, and then apply for a scholarship next year?"

She shakes her head. "You're talking about entry scholarships and they go directly from high school to university. There isn't the option of a year off – although that would make a great deal of sense for some students."

Sometimes she just seems like a machine that burps out answers. Press a button for question 1, and the answer is almost always 'no'. I don't know why I'm even bothering with this.

"Are there any scholarships for distance study courses? Like where you take stuff online?"

"I don't know of any – but I can look around." She looks at me for a minute, playing some kind of scenario in her mind. "You know, you could always register for a course somewhere, and get a part-time job. That way you could get your grade point average up. And if you're living at home…"

I cut her off. "No! I won't be living at home. I'm going somewhere else."

Miss Abel nods her head, like she knew this all along.

"How about a student loan? Can I get one of those?"

I know the answer even before she says anything. It's in her eyes. It's like a sign flashing on and off that says '*Loser*'.

"Well, thanks," I say, standing up. "Just wanted to check out some options."

She smiles, and for a minute, she turns human.

"If you want to do it, there's always a way. And you shouldn't give up on the scholarships. They don't all depend on high marks. Sometimes they reflect the personal quirks of the donor and you can qualify by being – oh, a left-handed bowler, or having Danish grandparents." She smiles at something. "I know a single mom who wanted to go to university, but she couldn't even think about it until her own daughter was grown up. Then she heard about a 'second chance' scholarship, set up by a woman whose husband didn't believe women should be educated. He died suddenly and left a large inheritance. She used part of it for her own education, and the rest for the scholarship." She laughs at the memory. "She won that argument." The smile fades and she focuses back in. "Obviously, that isn't going to work for you, because you aren't a mature student, but somewhere, I'm sure there's an award that can help you."

The interview is over. "Good luck," she smiles.

"Thanks," I mumble, as I walk out of the room. A minute later, I'm struck with a sudden thought. Could she have been telling me her own story? Nah. Couldn't be. But wouldn't that be a great plot for a book? Maybe I'll use it one day.

Meanwhile, I've got a real-life situation to deal with. When do I let Sahira in on the plan?

She's waiting to walk home with me. Just like we've done a thousand times since we started school. Just like we'll never do again, pretty soon. I'm feeling nostalgic already and she picks up on it.

"So what's wrong?"

"Nothing."

"Oh, come on, Christie. Something's bothering you. What is it?" She looks at me sort of sideways, then wrinkles her face up. "Is this still about me getting married?"

I shake my head. "Nope. I was just thinking about how many times we've walked home together. And how much I'm going to miss you when you're gone."

"It isn't forever. I'll come back."

"But it won't be the same."

She's quiet for a minute. "No," she says. "No. It won't."

We're both thinking about how things are going to be different. She'll have a husband – someone new in her life. And I'll have no one. She hasn't talked much about what she'll do after she's married – obviously, the plan is for him to work with her father. She'll probably find a job of some sort. At least, at first. Maybe that's why her parents bought that huge house a few years ago - I mean, who needs a five bedroom house for a family of three?

Sahira's words echo in my head. *"They must have planned it a long time ago."* Maybe they had. The prom dress that turned out to be a wedding dress and the house that's big enough for a second family. Who could have predicted that Sahira and her husband – assuming she'd found a husband by the normal method – would move in with Sahira's parents? No one. That's not what young couples do today. At least, normal newly-weds don't. But nothing about this situation is normal.

We walk the rest of the way in silence. She turns off at her house and I continue on to mine, where Tiffany's waiting for me, practically pouncing out from behind the door as I walk in.

"Who's William? And just where do you think you're going?"

Ah, yes. Karli has told her, of course. Anton thought the roundabout would divert her attention, but he doesn't know Tiffany. Of course she would have grilled Karli about our outing.

"He's just a guy at school. And where am I going? I don't know. I've been thinking seriously about taking a gap year before college."

There. I hadn't planned to tell her – I wanted to talk it over with Dad first. But she's going to find out anyway and just as predicted, she's livid.

"You're what? A gap year? To do what?"

"Broaden my horizons – maybe do a little travelling, think about what I want to do with the rest of my life."

She's working herself into a really good snit and it's almost laughable to see. Too bad they don't make silent movies any more. She'd be really great at that totally corny, over-the-wall style of acting.

"And just who do you think is going to pay for that?"

I smile. "Well, I haven't worked out all the details yet."

* * *

I see Anton the next morning at the end of the block. He's so wound up about something he walks part way up the block, then turns around to walk back with me. That's weird behavior, but he's all wound up about something.

"Have you sent in your application yet?" he asks me.

"For tree planting? No. Have you?"

He nods. "Yeah. My folks just about went ballistic."

"About tree planting? No shit."

He laughs. "No, not about the trees. About me going up to Kamloops. They want me to stay and take advanced courses during the summer so I can get a head start at university."

"They never give up, do they?"

"Nope. And they've sweetened the pot. Dad says he'll buy me a car. Not just a clunker, but a brand new one. A nice little KIA." He glances at me, sideways, with a little grin. "It's a pretty tempting offer."

"Oh, wow! Are you going to take it?"

He shakes his head. "Nope. I don't want to stay here and take summer courses. I'm just plain not interested. I want the summer off – and I want to earn my own money. I know I'll be back into science courses in the fall, but for the summer, I wanna do something else. And to be a little independent for a while."

We walk for a few minutes, before he breaks the silence.

"Having parents sucks."

"Tell me about it." We walk on a bit before I add, "I guess they're a necessary evil. I mean, we wouldn't be here if we didn't have them."

"I know, but it never seems to turn out right. I mean, look at my parents. They won't accept me as I am. And I can't spend the rest of my life pretending to be something else – or someone else, just to please them. Then there's Sahira's parents. Look at how they're messing up her life."

"You can throw my parents into the mix too," I say. "My mom's gone – my second mom, too. She seemed pretty nice, but it didn't work out. Then there was that train of temporary girl friends, but once Tiffany came on deck, my Dad just seems to have handed things over to her. Far as I can tell, her main objective seems to be screwing up my life. And I don't know why."

Anton paces along for a minute before he says anything. "There ought to be some other way. Like, maybe we could just grow in a lab somewhere and be set free when we're old enough."

"Maybe when you're a famous scientist you can figure out a way to do that." Then I laugh. "But quite honestly, I don't think I'd want to grow up in a test tube."

He looks at me for a minute. "Okay, maybe not exactly in a test tube. But wouldn't it be great if we did like some fishes do – the mom drops eggs somewhere, the dad squirts sperm on them, they swim away and the baby fishes never even see them again. Or if they do, they don't know it."

"You wanna be a fish?"

"Well, no. But maybe we could just grow in the ocean and then walk out onto the beach when we're ready. Just like evolution – at least, they think that's what happened a bajillion years ago. No parents. No problems. Wouldn't that be great?" He turns suddenly, and grabs my arm. "Hey – that could be a good book, couldn't it? Could you write that?"

While I'm thinking that over, he continues. "It would make a great TV series too. Really great. Lots of action. Brontosaurus or Tyrannus Rex or whoever, to battle when they come through the surf."

He punches the air. "Yowie! That would be so cool!"

I have to laugh. "Have you figured out who's going to star in the movie?"

Later that night, I think about his idea. Maybe it would work. Maybe I could write a book about it. Sci-fi is really popular right now. And almost everyone who has parents could relate to the idea of being totally free. The more I consider it, the more I like it.

CHAPTER EIGHT

DAD AND TIFFANY are celebrating their anniversary. Big deal. They're off to Red Robinson's on United Boulevard for the dinner show. Lots of former stars and used-to-be-big names on that circuit, but no one who's still popular today. Funny that Tiff even wants to go, because she's never seen most of the people who play there. Maybe it's the casino part that she likes – if she sits through the golden oldie show, she can go play in the casino afterwards. I laugh when I think of an old saying that's one of my dad's favourites: lucky in love, unlucky at cards. Or is it unlucky in love, lucky at cards? I wonder which Tiff thinks applies to her.

Whatever. As usual, I'm stuck baby-sitting Karli. I make dinner for the two of us – and promise myself that when I'm on my own, I'll never eat Kraft dinner again. But Karli loves it. We watch some video cartoons for a while and pretty soon it's her bedtime. I scoot her into the tub for a bubble bath, tuck her into bed and I've got the whole evening ahead of me to do nothing. And do it all by myself. No Saturday night dates for me. No nothing when you get right down to it.

I'm in a really bitchy mood – probably one of the times I should go out for a run or something, but I can't. Not when I have to look after Karli.

There's nothing decent on TV. There's nothing to read. I don't even want to go raid Dad's liquor cabinet. Been there, done that. Getting stinking drunk doesn't solve anything and just leaves me with a headache.

Karli mutters something in her sleep and I sit with her a while, rubbing her back. She finally drifts off again and I tip toe out of the room. Dad and Tiff's bedroom door is open and I stop to look in. What a mess! Looks like half the stuff in her closet is piled up on the bed. Probably trying to figure out what to wear - which, far as I know, she'd already solved by buying a new dress to wear tonight.

Oh, yeah, I remind myself. This is the same lady that got so uptight at the suggestion of me taking a gap year. If she cut back even a quarter on what she spends on herself, there wouldn't be a problem.

Curious, I step into the room. Normally, it's closed. In our house, a closed door is as good as locked, and I've never had occasion to go into their bedroom before. Never wanted to, really. I guess I never wanted to admit to myself what she and dad were doing in there. I mean, I know Karli isn't an Immaculate Conception, but still – the whole idea is pretty disgusting.

Tiffany has one of those celebrity dressing tables. It's about waist high and comes in three parts with a set of drawers on either side and a huge circular mirror and a dresser top in the middle. There's a whole whack of makeup dumped front of the mirror. It's like she thinks she's a movie star or something. A pretty messy movie star at that – or maybe she thinks she ought to have someone to clean up after her. I sit on the pink, padded bench in front of the dressing table and look at myself in the mirror.

I'm no raving beauty, but it could be worse. I pick up one of her eyebrow pencils, then put it down. I'm not really into this stuff. As I turn away from the mirror, I notice one of the drawers isn't quite closed and reach my hand out towards it. I honestly mean to close it, but my hand seems to be working all by itself and pulls the drawer open. There's a tangled mess of lingerie in it. If I had that kind of stuff I'd sure look after it better than she does. I pick up a couple of pieces – nothing much to them. Just bits of lace and embroidery. Whoops! Here's some fancy thong underwear. I hold it up to the mirror and laugh at the image.

While I'm putting it back, my hand delves deeper in the drawer and dredges up a book. It's some sort of diary by the looks of it. Should I open it? No. Of course not. Will I? Hell yes!

Wow! It goes back years. I thumb back to the early pages – it seems to start back when she was just finishing high school. Blah, blah, blah – all the usual high school stuff, then it switches to the summer where she's doing an internship of some sort. Seems to be involved with marketing and conventions. I guess that's where she met my dad.

My phone rings. It's Sahira.

"Wuzzup girl friend?"

"Just wondered if you could come over. Nothing special."

"Wish I could. I've got Karli duty tonight. Dad and Tiff have gone out for the evening."

"So what are you doing?"

"You wouldn't believe it."

Now her voice comes to life. "What? Come on. Tell."

"I just happened to open Tiff's lingerie drawer and found her diary."

There's a fast intake of breath on the other end of the line.

"Did you look at it?"

"Oh, no," I say. "I'm just sitting here admiring the cover."

Sahira giggles.

"Any good stuff?"

"Just coming to it."

I start reading at random.

> *Worked late tonight. Mitch took me to dinner and drove me home after. I invited him up to my apartment. It was everything I'd hoped for.*

"Oh, Jeez. What a slut! I can't believe my dad was taken in by someone like that. There's more," I add, continuing to read.

> *Another convention with Mitch. This was all about marketing – not actually selling anything but learning how to do it. School seems such a waste of time compared to on-the-job experience like this. Mitch and I had a wonderful weekend. I know he truly loves me.*

I flip back a few more pages and my eyes blink as I take in what she's written. I'm so stunned I can't even read the entry to Sahira. It takes me a minute to get to the next line. She's written a comment, and then scratched double lines under it. They're written so hard they've almost gone through the page. I read the line again to myself: *I absolutely hate Donald. What a pig.*

"So – what's next? Come on. Don't stop now."

"Just some junk about Donald. What she says is she hates Donald, because he's a real pig."

"Who's Donald?" Sahira asks.

"I dunno. Oh, darn. Gotta go. Karli's calling."

That's a lie, but it's a good excuse to end the conversation. I open the book again. It takes me a minute to find the page, but when I do, the words jump out at me. I re-read the first line. It's easy to find, with all the double underlining. Then I let myself read the next line: *Just because we went all the way a couple of times, he seems to think he can do it whenever he wants. And he doesn't even bring anything to use.*

I move forward a few more pages. She's on about her job again, and about shopping with a girlfriend, then comes a series of exclamation marks. *I hope this isn't what I think it is. I don't want to marry Donald – he's a dork. But if Mitch thinks it's his....* I slam the book shut and shove it back into the drawer, under her lingerie.

Shit. Now what? Do I tell Dad that Karli might not even be his kid? Would it matter? I don't care if Tiffany gets kicked out, but I'd hate to think of her being a single mom to Karli. She's so bloody irresponsible and uncaring. She treats Karli more like some kind of a pet than a real person. Karli needs Dad. She needs a real mom too, but that's not going to happen.

I take a last look around the room. Where exactly was the eyebrow pencil? Is everything the way it was before I came in? The door clicks behind me before I remember the drawer was partially open. I tip-toe back into the room re-open the drawer and leave the door just a little ajar behind me. Perfect. She'll never know.

That night, I can't help thinking about my real mom. I was so young when she died. Not quite four years old. I never thought about it before, but that's almost how old Karli is now. Most of what I remember about my mom is her singing to me. And laughing while we played games together. I've seen pictures of her and she was really pretty – soft, blond hair, big blue eyes and always, the sweetest expression on her face. Sometimes she was smiling – in most of the pictures actually – but even when she wasn't, she still looked happy.

I guess the good fairies had a day off when I was born, because they sure weren't hovering over my cradle. I didn't turn out pretty, blond or blue-eyed like my mom. I take after my Dad's side of the family, which seems to be exclusively dark brown hair, and dark eyes. At least, that's what it seems like in the few pictures that I have seen. I never really got to know any of my dad's relatives. I don't know why, but Dad was never close to his family. They all lived back east, in one of the suburbs of Toronto. We never went there, and they never came here, so I never met any of them in person. Well, that was their tough luck too, because they never got to meet me either. We used to get letters from them at Christmas, sometimes with a cheque inside and once in a while, a picture. That lasted for a few Christmases, and then we never heard from them again. I don't even know if my grandparents are still alive.

That's the pits. Really and truly rotten. What kind of family is this anyway? Maybe things would have been better for dad if they'd been somewhere in the vicinity to give him a little support and a little love when the going got tough with mom. Just plain, old-fashioned love. From what I can see, except for mom, that's something he's never had much of.

It wasn't much better on the other side of the family. I don't know anything about my mom's family – not their names, or where they lived, or anything about them. Maybe mom told me but I was still a little girl when she died, and if she did say anything, I don't remember it. I don't know, maybe mom and dad eloped or something? A true love match. Yeah. That's sort of warm and fuzzy to think about. And it could explain why their families cut them off. It's easier to believe that than to think my grandparents were real pricks. But it would be interesting to find out something about my ancestors. Who knows, some of them might even be famous.

I really missed my mom when I was little. Dad tried hard, but he had to work, and he never seemed to be able to find a baby-sitter that lasted. I guess what we needed was an old-fashioned Nanny, like Mary Poppins or something, but instead, he got married again. Her name was Jeanette and the first thing she said to me was, "I'm going to be your new mom. I know we'll have fun together." Well, I didn't want a new mom. I wanted my *own* mom, and she wasn't it. Plus she didn't know diddly squat about little girls. Her idea of having fun was taking me out shopping with her. Jeez, what is it with some women and shopping? Like it's a national sport or something. *Flash* Earth to Jeanette. Five year old girls aren't shopping fanatics. Especially when the shopping trip involves *your* stuff, with maybe a last-minute toy purchase thrown in to appease the kid.

Anyway, me and Jeanette never really got along. Now that I think about it, her and dad never got along very much either. Not even at the beginning when it should have been all lovey-dovey. Most of my memories of Jeanette have to do with fighting, yelling at my dad, throwing stuff at the walls, and crying. Lots of crying. She didn't last very long. After that, there was a string of live-in girlfriends – some stayed for a while, but mostly they moved on pretty quick. I learned right from the start, not to get attached to any of them, because whatever they had in mind when they moved in with my dad, it didn't involve looking after a little kid so they moved out. It sometimes felt like I was on one of the moving walkways in the mall, going around in circles for hours and never getting anywhere. Move in, move out. Move in, move out. It got so there wasn't even any point in trying to remember their names. So I didn't. I just called most of them 'Hey'. And I never paid much attention to anything they said. I must have been a real bratty kid because no one wanted me then. And no one seems to want me now. Not any of my relatives, and certainly not Tiffany.

Well, that's not completely true. There's always been my dad. He's always been great. I know he loves me and he always has, but when Tiffany moved in, things really changed. She goes bananas if he spends too much time with me. Now that I think of it, she goes bananas if he spends too much time with anyone – other than her. But lately, even that seems to have changed.

It won't be hard to move out.

I take out the application form Anton downloaded for me and look at it carefully. Time to send it in and get the show on the road.

CHAPTER NINE

SOMEHOW, IT'S JUNE. The exam schedule is posted and I feel like I'm at the starting line of a race. A very long race. A race I don't have a hope in hell of winning. Everything takes on new drama, like some weird kind of fantasy set in a distant galaxy.

This will be the last time I write final exams. I don't know how to feel about that. In one way it's a relief because I hate exams. I mean, they're so pointless. Who cares if I know when the Battle of Hastings took place? Isn't it more important to know how global warming is taking place – and what we're doing about it? Or not doing about it? I mean, some of the stuff they ask on exams isn't going to ever be useful in real life. So to me, exams are just a waste of time. And while I'll be happy to have all my exams over with, it's going to be a downer because it means the end of school, and that means the end of a lot of friendships, and the end of predictable times. There's a third theme to my thoughts as well – why am I even bothering to write exams since the results don't mean anything to anybody? I might dream about going to university, but it ain't gonna happen. Not to me. Not in this lifetime. So why don't I just head for the beach, give myself a little extra holiday, work on my summer tan and let the brainiacs wrestle with the tests and quizzes and essays. I'm sure the teachers would be happy to have one less set of exams to mark.

I may not be a whiz at school, but I'm feeling pretty good about myself otherwise. Anton's conditioning program was a killer at first. I mean, I absolutely hated it. We hiked up and down Citadel Hill so many times that I was beginning to feel like some kind of machine.

"Screw this," I told him, early in his programme, when he came to the house to pick me up for one of our sessions. "It's raining. I'm not going out and get soaking wet for nothing."

"It isn't for nothing. And it rains during the summer – even in Kamloops. You gotta be ready."

The next day, he has a surprise for me. He'd told me to bring along the backpack I bought a week ago at the Thrift Shop. "New ones are too expensive," he said. "And they're only going to get all grubby anyway when we get out in the bush. So don't waste your money. Check out the used ones."

That made sense. Not taking a good backpack in the bush was a no-brainer, but we weren't going out in the bush yet. "What do I need a backpack for in the park?"

"You'll see."

I do. He's brought his pack too and he loads both of them up with two pairs of four-litre milk jugs. He unloads them and takes them to the water tap to fill.

"What's that for?" I have the horrible feeling that I know exactly what he's going to do with them. Correction. What we're going to do.

"We need to get used to hiking with loads in our packs."

How do you say thank you to someone for something you don't want? "Okay. Let's get it over with."

With two jugs filled with water, my pack weighs a ton. Easy. The hill I thought I had conquered loomed like a mini Mt. Everest today, daring me to make light of it.

"You'll thank me when we get to Kamloops," Anton laughs as we chug our way up from Shaughnessy Street.

"Sure I will," I gasp. "All I have to do is live that long."

How come he isn't wheezing and gasping too? Jeez – has he been doing this all along? Why haven't I ever noticed what good shape he's in? Probably because he doesn't look like a Mr. Muscleman. No bulging biceps, no telephone pole thighs. But underneath the jeans and loose T-shirts, there's a pretty fit body. Lean and mean. I laugh to myself. *Really* mean.

When we reach the park at the top of the hill, we stop for a water break before galloping down the other side, then turn around and do it all over again. Over the next few days we repeat this, varying the route by taking the bridge over the bypass and making a figure eight out of the run, or looping around at the top of the hill to include the elementary school grounds in our circuit. That makes it twice as long, but Anton's right. It does get easier. Not that I'll admit that to him. While we're sitting in the park taking a break after our final hill sprints, Anton asks the question I've been dreading.

"What's happening with Sahira?"

"Nothing yet. Will you help me talk to her?"

He shakes his head. "Nope. That whole thing is your baby."

He's right, of course. The other thing I have to do is tell my dad about Kamloops, so that night, after dinner, I decide the time is right.

"Dad, can we talk?" I can almost see Tiffany's ears perk up.

"Sure. What's up?"

"About this summer." He waits, as I search for words. "I'm thinking about working for the summer."

Tiffany smirks. Like she cares. I ignore her and continue talking to dad. "They're hiring tree planters in Kamloops. It pays pretty good."

He looks at me. "Tree planting is hard work."

"I know, but I think I can do it."

"Maybe for the summer, but then what?"

"I want to take a year off to write."

Tiffany butts in. "Oh, come on. That's just …" Dad gives her a look that shuts her up.

"Living on my own will be good experience – learning to look after myself and everything."

The silence deepens. I'm trying to read Dad's face – but I can't. Finally he speaks.

"I guess I have to face the fact that my little girl is growing up. But she'll always be my little girl." He smiles. "If that's what you want to do, you can give it a try. If you need an allowance, I can help out."

Tiffany stiffens, registering her protest. Right. Give me an allowance? That might cut into her spending.

"What about Karli?" She's almost hissing now. "She's your sister, after all. Doesn't she deserve some consideration?"

I look at her and have to bite back the words before they slip out of my mouth. She isn't my sister, and I want Tiffany to know that I know that.

"Ah yes." I throw in the longest pause I can get away with and look straight at Tiffany. "Yes, indeed. My *sister*. We have to consider my *sister*, don't we?"

Her eyes flare. Yes! She got the message.

It's obvious my dad doesn't know that Karli is a cuckoo in the nest, but he loves her, and I don't want to hurt him. For now, just letting Tiffany know is enough. I turn back to my dad.

"I'd like to do it on my own, if I can. But thanks for the offer."

"It's there anytime you need it."

My dad really is the greatest.

* * *

Anton is on my case again the next day as we slog up the hill and around circuit with loaded backpacks. My lungs no longer threaten to collapse, but a breather and a water break is still welcome.

"So, have you talked to Sahira yet?"

"No." Before he can say anything, I jump in. "I'll see her tonight."

"Great. Let me know what happens."

When I reach Sahira's house later that day, her mom answers the door, as always, and shows me in with a smile, as always. But when I look at her a little more closely, I start to wonder. Is that really a smile? Or is she just being polite? Whatever. She smiles again and points upstairs, meaning Sahira is in her room. All she ever does is smile and point, and for the first time, I wonder if she even speaks English? Is that even possible? *Jeez – what else don't I know about this family?* I smile back and mount the familiar staircase. Each step seems higher and more difficult than the last.

"Hi!" Sahira's face lights up. "What's up?"

"Just thought I'd drop in." Even as I say the words, I can hear how lame they sound. I never 'just drop in'. We always text first.

"So. What's happening?"

What to say? Are you still planning to get married? Wanna reconsider and run away? My great plan is floating away, stranded by my lack of words.

She walks toward me. "What's the matter? What's wrong?"

"It's just… Sahira." I take a deep breath and start again. "You getting married just seems so wrong."

She looks at me for a moment. "I thought we finished talking about that."

"Not really. There are options."

"Like what?" It's a question, but you can tell she doesn't really think there's an answer.

"Like – like not doing it."

She turns away and mumbles her answer. "That isn't an option."

I take a breath. It's now or never. "Look, me and Anton are going to Kamloops for the summer – tree planting."

"Yeah, I know. Sounds like an interesting project, and I know how hard you and Anton have been working, getting ready for it. I hope everything works out for you."

"No, wait. There's more. We thought…" Damn. How do I say this? She's giving me a funny look already – the eyebrows are quirking up, questioning something. She knows something is brewing, but doesn't yet know what it is. Oh, shit. I take a deep breath and plunge in. "We thought you could come with us. Move to Kamloops and then you could use that Thompson River University scholarship that you won."

She looks at me blankly, before she shakes her head. "In case you've forgotten, I'll be in the Punjab, getting married. And even if I wasn't, that deadline for accepting that scholarship is 'way passed."

"Well, no, it isn't."

Her eyebrows shoot up. "What do you mean?"

"It's like…" I bite my lips, searching for the right words. "Sahira, I did something. You might get mad, but it seemed the right thing to do."

Her look says it all. This is not going to be easy.

"I accepted that scholarship."

"Why? They won't let you use it."

"No. I accepted it for you. I thought if that option was open, you could use it if you changed your mind."

"If I changed my mind? Just how do you think I might do that?"

Oh, god. This is getting harder by the second. "You don't have to go marry some guy you've never met."

She looks up, as though waiting for a magical response to appear on the ceiling.

I charge ahead. "I mean, you can stay with me and Anton and go to school. You can still be a vet." The silence solidifies. "That is if that's still what you want to do." I finish, lamely. My words drag to a halt. Oh, shit. This isn't working the way I thought it would. I somehow figured she'd jump up, give me a hug and shed tears of relief. Well, okay, maybe that's being overdramatic. But I thought she'd at least consider it. Now I know it was a crummy idea. All I'm accomplishing is pissing off a friend. She'll probably never speak to me again.

She takes a deep breath. "I can't do that. It would shame my father."

"But how about you? It's your life."

Her words are patient and almost pitying. "You still don't understand."

"No, I don't understand. I don't understand any of this. You sit there, all locked up inside yourself, saying nothing, doing nothing. Nothing seems to penetrate, nothing seems to matter. This is your *life*, Sahira."

Her eyes seem larger than ever, and somehow gentler. She starts to speak, but I interrupt.

"Don't you care about any of this? If it was me, I'd be so fucking mad I'd be kicking and screaming and putting my fist through the walls. And I'd blow my top if someone like me tried to mess around with my life, but nothing seems to get through to you.

"Sahira, just for once, think about yourself. You don't live in India, you live here. You're Canadian. You don't have to follow rules from somewhere else."

She takes a breath, but I bulldoze ahead, cutting her off.

"You've got a great scholarship. You have two friends who want to help you. Yes, I know, your dad will be mad – but he'll get over it." That's when her eyes stop being all mellow, and she shakes her head.

"It's your life, Sahira. It's time for you to take control of it."

There's nothing more to say. I leave the room, wondering if I've put an end to a life-long friendship. Wondering if she'll even consider what I'd said. Wondering if I'll ever see her again.

When I reach the foot of the stairs, her mother smiles and waves to me from the kitchen. That eternal damn kitchen. What the hell does she do there all day? No one eats that much. Not even the people who come to the Gurdwara for their free lunches.

I smile, wave back and let myself out.

CHAPTER TEN

IF I BELIEVED in fairy godmothers, I'd have to admit that Christie would be perfect in the role. She's been thinking about me, and about my problem. And I only wish I could do what she suggested. Walk away from everything, just go up to Kamloops, go to university and make a life for myself.

No more listening to my dad yelling and screaming. No more having to cover up bruises and sores from where he's hit me.

No more watching him browbeat my mother, and watching her cringe when he gets mad.

Then I stop. What would happen if I did leave?

Nothing. Nothing would happen. Nothing would change. I can't stop him from picking on her. And if I can't do anything by being here, it isn't going to get any worse if I'm not here.

Somehow, someone has to do something for my mom and it looks like that someone will have to be me. Now I have some serious thinking to do.

"No, damn it." I'm talking out loud now. "Thinking about it isn't enough. Somehow, I have to do something about it."

I nod my head. Yes. I do have to do something. And I have to do it fast.

For a minute I think about asking her to come to Kamloops with me. That might work, mightn't it?

Then I realize there's no way it could happen. First, she probably wouldn't come. Second, that would mean involving Christie and Anton if she was going to stay with us. And then I remember, the scholarship included a room in the dorm so I won't be staying with Christie and Anton. There's no way my mom could stay at the university with me. And there's no way I could dump her on Christie and Anton. Then I laugh. I don't even have any idea where they will be staying – whether they'll be together or get separate places or whatever. And anyway, there's no way I could afford to support my mom.

No, there has to be another solution.

But what?

CHAPTER ELEVEN

"HEY," ANTON CALLS. "Slow down! We're not racing."

I laugh. What a change from when we started all this, and I could barely stagger up the hill. Now I'm trotting with a weighted backpack and I'm hardly even winded. We crest the hill, and jog slowly into the park before we hit our final lap. It's the middle of June. Exams are almost over and after that, all we have left to do at school is go in to pick up our final reports.

"Well, I did it," I tell Anton, as we stretch our hamstrings. "I talked to Sahira last night."

"And?"

"Nothing. She won't even consider it. I guess I was way out in left field on this one. But I really thought she'd go for it."

"Pretty hard for her, though. I mean, she's never stood up to her father about anything, has she?"

Maybe she had, maybe she hadn't. My impression, like Anton's, is that she'd always done what she was told. I mean, she's such a quiet person. Nice, sweet and all those other gooey adjectives, but not someone who would be a shit disturber. Even mildly.

I have to agree with him. "No. But this would have been a great place to start."

"So what happens now?"

I shrug. "Nothing, I guess. You and I can still do the tree-planting gig, and then we'll just have to see what happens after that. I told dad I might stay in Kamloops for a year to write. It would be easier than trying to do it at home. Tiffany's always after me to do stuff. And she's not the most encouraging person to be around. Dad would be great but Tiff would be a real pain in the ass. She thinks my life-time job should be baby-sitting Karli." I kick a rock off the pavement. "Now I don't know what's going to happen."

Anton looks at me. It's a look that speaks volumes. "Weird, isn't it. Your problem is that your parents don't really seem to care about you and what you want to do. Well – not your dad, but your mom."

I practically spit my words out. "She's not my mom, Anton. She's nothing to me. I don't give a shit what she thinks about anything. It's my dad I'm thinking about. He's always been the greatest."

"Sorry – I didn't mean that the way it sounded. I just meant you didn't have ..." his words trickle off. Then he starts again. "Sahira's parents don't seem to consider her at all. Far as I can tell, they never even asked her if she wanted to get married. Just told her." He pauses, tracing a pattern on his kneecap with his thumb. He shakes his head. "Then there's my parents. They'll do anything I want -anything but let me be who I really am."

He sighs, picks up his pack and slings it on his back. "Come on. Let's finish our run."

* * *

That evening, I look around my room, trying to figure out what I need to take with me. Sorting stuff is always a challenge – some things I know I should throw out or put out for recycling, but it's really hard to do. I can't get rid of anything from my mom. My real mom. I don't have hardly anything of hers. Just a couple of silly things – like her hairbrush. It's a pretty one, with mother-of-pearl backing. I never use it, but sometimes I take it out and just hold it, like I can still feel something of her clinging to it. I've got a bracelet that used to be hers too. I never wear it – but sometimes I take it out and look at it. Is it just my imagination, or can the essence of a person really cling to objects that they've used? Somehow, it makes me feel better to think that's true. I put the brush and the bracelet to one side. I can do them up in bubble-wrap and they won't take up much room in the bottom of my pack. They can be my own personal talisman. Stupid to think that way I suppose, but sometimes I need a little backup.

I put a few things down on the 'pack' pile and look at the rest of the stuff in my closet that has to be sorted out. I haul out the boxes I've been saving for the past couple of months. I'd flattened them out and stored them under my bed. Now I restore them to their original shape and slap a couple of layers of duct tape across the bottoms. I decide to start with the things I'll need next winter. I can ask Dad to send them up to me later, but for now, I want to get everything sorted, cleared away and stored away. I know if I leave it here, there's a good chance Tiffany will junk everything in my room. She keeps yapping about a sewing room. Not that she ever sews anything. At least, nothing I've ever seen. But still, she thinks it would be neat to have a sewing room to keep all her stuff in. Or at least, that's what she says. I think she's been looking at too many home decorating magazines. It's amazing how much 'stuff' I've accumulated. Some of it I've outgrown and I can't imagine why I'm still keeping it. Some of it's waaaay out of style, and I'll never wear it except maybe as part of a Hallowe'en costume or some other dress-up gig.

When I finish with the closet, I start emptying out my dresser drawers. My stack of boxes has evolved into four piles. Must Have in Kamloops. Must Go To The Thrift Shop. Send Later. Maybe.

The Must Have pile is stuff I'll wear every day. The information booklet Anton gave me says that planting trees can be really hot work. So – should I take shorts? Or, since it's out in the bush, would jeans be better? I'll have to check that out but for now, I put both jeans and shorts in the Must Have pile.

I've got some raggedy old tee-shirts that I'll be happy to wear and toss out. There are a few new ones, wicking fabrics that will be great for hot days. But maybe I'll need long sleeved sweat shirts for the bush so my arms don't get all scratched up? Something else to put on my 'check it out' list. I sort through my underwear drawer, looking for practical stuff. I'll leave the lacy thongs and the strapless bras for dad to send up later. Socks. Lots of socks. They wear out quickly in heavy boots. Then I look at the socks again. Most of them are for wearing with tennis shoes. They're low cut, just barely grazing the ankle. I've only got one pair of boot socks and those are left over from my ski boots. They probably won't be too good either. I'll have to get a few pairs of proper boot socks. I grab a pencil and start a list, under the heading 'Things To Get'.

Then I realize, I won't be working every day. At least, I think there will be days off. Maybe I'll need a couple of dressier outfits – not dress up, but just not ragged stuff. I sort through the piles again, shuffling things from one stack to another.

I'm just about finished, when my phone rings. I smile every time I hear it – my ringtone is *I'm Off To See The Wizard* – I love that song. I glance at the call indicator. It's Sahira.

"Hey girl, what's up."

Her voice shocks me. "I can't," she sobs. "I can't."

"What's wrong? Sahira, what's happening?"

I can hardly figure out what she's saying, she's crying so hard that her words are all mashed together. "Hey, Sahira – stop. I can't understand you. Come on, girlfriend. Take a deep breath and start again." She does. Her breathing is still ragged, but if I'm hearing right, she wants me to meet her at the park. That's crazy – she's never allowed out at night, and it's almost 10 o'clock now.

Then her voice comes through loud and clear. "Please. You have to help me."

"Okay, girlfriend. Calm down. I'm leaving the house right now. Hang on, it's going to be okay."

"Don't tell...." Her voice trails off into more sobs. I don't know who I'm not supposed to tell, or what, but she needs me right now. "Hey girl, hang in there. I'm on my way." It takes two minutes to shove my feet into a pair of shoes, grab a jacket and fly down stairs.

"Hey, Dad, I'm going out for a few minutes."

He glances at his watch. "Okay, but don't be too late."

Tiffany just glares.

When I get to the park, Sahira's sitting on one of the swings, slumped over like all the bones have been extracted from her body.

"Hey, girlfriend! What's up?"

She launches herself at me, and starts crying again. There's only one response. A big hug.

"It's all right, girlfriend. It's going to be okay. Whatever it is, we can fix it."

"No, you can't."

I lead her over to a bench. "Here – sit down. Now, tell me what's happened?"

"I told my dad I didn't want to get married."

Oh Jeez. I can just imagine what happened. But I need to know what he's done.

"And?" I ask, putting my arm around her.

She winces, and pulls away. "He said it didn't matter if I wanted to or not. All the arrangements had been made. And anyway, life wasn't like the movies. Marriages were arranged for a reason – to build alliances, and stuff like that.

"I told him this wasn't the Middle Ages, and we weren't playing politics or trying to usurp a throne somewhere."

Wow! This girl comes up with the most amazing things at times. "Usurp a throne?"

She giggles through her tears. "Yeah – that's what I said."

"So now what?"

Her face clouds up again and she pulls her sweater sleeves down over her hands. "He..." She clenches her hands together and takes a deep breath. "He shoved me into my room and locked the door. He said I could just stay there until I came to my senses."

Holy shit! This sounds more and more like a silent movies melodrama. Does anyone really do things like that today? I guess they do. I look at her for a long minute. After all the discussions we've had, all the arguments about whether she should do it or not, something must have happened.

"I don't get it. How come you changed your mind?"

She looks at me for a long minute before her face crumples and the tears start to flow. Between sobs, it finally comes out. She'd asked him how long she would have to stay in India before she could come back home and start the sponsorship program for her new husband.

"He said I could come home when I was pregnant with a son."

My stomach clenches just hearing that. How must Sahira have felt?

"Oh, Jeez. Sahira. That's so awful."

Then I thought about some of the things she'd said – like, her father knowing what was best for her. That doesn't fit with what she's telling me now.

I put my arm around her shoulders. "Hey. It's going to be okay."

But the sobs continue. "No it isn't," she says.

I hand her a Kleenex. She takes it, and blows a mighty honk. Then she laughs.

"You must think I'm pretty stupid."

"Not exactly stupid – but you're a big girl. You know what marriage entails."

She wads up the Kleenex and tosses it in a nearby trash basket, like she's stalling for time – trying to decide what to say.

"Yeah. I know what marriage entails. But I really thought it was just about getting married to get some kind of legal stuff, so his cousin could come to Canada, like a paper marriage or something. Just going through the motions. Not a real marriage. I couldn't tell you that – I couldn't tell anyone, because my dad would get in real trouble if anybody found out. I mean, you read about that stuff all the time and there's some big time fines and jail sentences when they catch people. But he'd never said anything about it, and I was started to get a little scared. When I told him I didn't want to get married, I was sure that was when he'd tell me it would all be okay – it wasn't a real marriage. Just going through the motions so his cousin could come to Canada. But he didn't say that, or anything like it. What he said was, I could come home when I was pregnant with a son. It just hit me then, what lay ahead. There wouldn't be an annulment or an easy divorce or anything after his cousin arrived – this was going to be the real thing. And 'with a son' meant I might have to stay there for years. And I knew I couldn't do it."

"How'd you get out?"

"I climbed out the window."

"You what?" This is definitely a new Sahira. That's not something the old one would have ever done. So – what comes next? What do we do now?

"You can stay at my place," I tell her.

"No. I can't do that. I don't want him to know where I am. Not that he'll care."

"Of course he'll care," I say, but she cuts me off.

"No. He won't. He's hated me since the day I was born. I wasn't a boy."

Sometimes I really don't understand Sahira. How could she live with that? Thinking her father hates her? It isn't the first time she's said it. I put the thought away. Right now, it doesn't matter what he thinks. She needs help.

"Do you have any money?"

I know the minute I ask, what the answer will be. Of course not. Her dad keeps her on a really tight string. Her mom, too. She told me once her mom had to give him the weekly shopping list, and he'd go over it, crossing out stuff he didn't think she needed before he gave her money for what he'd approved. I couldn't imagine my dad doing anything like that – not to my mom, not to my step-mom, not to the string of girlfriends who'd moved in with him – and not even with Tiffany. Especially not with Tiffany.

Sahira hasn't brought anything with her but I can lend her some jeans and tee-shirts. They'll be loose on her, but that won't matter.

"Come back to my place. You can stay with me tonight and we'll figure out what to do tomorrow."

She shakes her head. "I can't do that."

I stand up. "My Dad's expecting me home. We gotta go."

She starts to protest but I silence her with a wave. "Stop saying 'no'. Move it."

When we get to the house, she doesn't want to come in, and I'm tired of arguing so I send her around to the back patio. It's sheltered, safe, and there's comfortable stuff there for her to sit on.

Once in the house, I find my father. "Dad – I really need to talk to you. Alone." I don't know where Tiffany is, but I do know I don't want her involved in this.

He follows me to the kitchen. "It's about Sahira. Her dad has her signed her up to get married to some guy in India that she's never even met."

"But – he can't…"

"Yeah, it seems he can. At least, Sahira thinks he can. She just told him that she doesn't want to do it and he locked her in her room. Said she can't come out until she agrees to do it."

My Dad takes a deep breath. "My God! That's unbelievable."

"There's more." I tell him about the scholarship, the plans Anton and I had made, to stay with Jeff in Kamloops, until we can find a place for the two of us to stay.

"You mean Tiffany is right about Anton? And you're going to elope?"

"Not funny, Dad. I never said anything, because it was such a huge joke to listen to Tiffany rant about him. Anton's gay. There's absolutely nothing to worry about on that score. We're just good friends."

He laughs. "That's really funny."

"Yeah. Well, right now, Sahira's the problem. She can stay with me and Anton once we get settled in Kamloops, but first we have to get her up there."

"But won't her dad…"

I cut him off. "Her dad doesn't know anything about the scholarship. Kamloops is the last place he'd think of looking for her."

"So what happens now?"

"She doesn't have any money. I've got a few bucks saved up – she can have that – but I don't know how much she'll need for bus fare and stuff."

My Dad is quiet for a minute, mulling something over. Then he smiles, like he's figured out a plan of action.

"When were you planning to go to Kamloops?"

"I hadn't set a definite date - My last exam is tomorrow, but the results won't be out for another week or so. I don't have to stay here to get them – they'll mail them out. I guess that means I could leave any time after tomorrow."

He smiles.

"I'm assuming Sahira still has a final exam?"

"Yes. We're both writing the same exam tomorrow."

"She could leave tomorrow? Or the next day?"

I nod. "Yep. I think she'd be glad to get going. She could stay here for a couple of days but that might not be such a good idea. It's would be too obvious to her dad – I mean, he'd probably be pounding on our door right now if he knew she wasn't still locked in her room."

Dad looks at me for a long minute. "So where is she now?"

I point. "She's out in the patio. She didn't want to come in."

"Well, she doesn't have to worry about me. She's welcome here." He pauses. "Does she want me to talk to her dad? Do you think it would help at all?"

"I think that's the last thing she wants. But maybe if he comes looking for her, you could try to reason with him."

Dad shakes his head, sadly. "I don't think that's a very real possibility, somehow. I don't know too much about it – other than what I've read – but if she's disobeyed him, she's pretty much out of his life."

Out of his life? "Are you serious?"

"I'm afraid so. Anyway, we don't have to worry about that now. Go get Sahira. We'll sort it out tomorrow." He pauses. "I'll tell Tiff that we've got company."

I start to protest, but there's no point. She'll have to know – I just don't want her meddling around. "Okay – but don't tell her about Anton."

He laughs. "Not a word."

That night, when Sahira's changing into a pair of my pjs, I notice a series of bruises across her back. Old bruises with an overlay of newer welts. It looks like someone's taken a belt to her back.

"Holy shit – what happened?"

"Just me being clumsy. I tripped and fell on the stairs."

Sahira tripped? Again? I'm finding her excuses harder and harder to believe. She's one of the most graceful people I know. And you don't get those kinds of bruises from skidding on the stairs. Not layers of bruises like that. It's obvious she doesn't want to talk about it, and this doesn't seem like the time. I rummage around in the bathroom and find a toothbrush that's still in its wrapper. I laugh to myself. We shop at Costco and seem to have a dozen of everything. But sometimes it comes in handy – like now.

"Here," I say, handing her the brush and a tube of toothpaste. "We've got extras."

Then she smiles. It's the first real smile I've seen all evening. "I'm lucky to have such a good friend."

Oh, shit. Now she's going to get all mushy. "Yeah – well, if there's anything you need, let me know. We've got enough stuff around here to outfit an army."

* * *

I don't know how Sahira gets through her last exam with all the crap that's going on in her life – and especially now. I'm amazed that she can remember anything, but she says it isn't hard. I guess when you're an A+ student, exams aren't a problem. It's just ordinary mortals like me who find them a challenge. We finish our exams, come home and pack a few things. Tiff was real weird when she found out Sahira was going to stay with us for a couple of days, but then she actually got quite pleasant and tried to help Sahira. I'm not sure if she was really concerned about Sahira or she was just looking forward to getting rid of me.

Karli comes into my room while we're packing, and offers Sahira one of her teddy bears to take with her on the bus.

"Thank you," Sahira smiles, bending down to give Karli a hug. "But I couldn't take your favourite teddy bear."

Karli considers for a minute. "He's not my favourite, but he's my almost favourite."

We laugh – one of the few times I'd seen Sahira look happy since I brought her home. After breakfast, Dad slips me a cheque just before we get in the car to drive to the bus depot.

"Here, kiddo. Tuck this in your wallet," he instructs. "Open a bank account once you're settled, and send me the information, so I can make a deposit if I have any left-over money that I need to get rid of."

I start to protest, but he isn't having any of it. "Just do as you're told, for once. Otherwise I'll have to kick you out of the house, too."

Dad's trying to make a joke of it, and at some other time it might have been funny, but I could almost feel Sahira cringe when he said it. He drives us to the bus depot, and stays with us until we're safely on board.

We're lucky and find seats at the front of the bus on the left hand side, right behind the driver. That means we get a great view.

I'm looking forward to the trip to Kamloops. The Fraser Valley is interesting, but nothing new. When dad was a kid, his family used to go to the Chilliwack Cherry Festival every year on July 1st. That's was sort of their official start to summer. They don't have the festival any more, but dad and I go out there on July 1st every year anyway. The cherries are at their peak and we gorge on them. Now Tiff and Karli come too – Karli loves it, and gobbles up the cherries. Tiff complains the whole time. I don't know why she even bothers coming. Anyway, I've been as far as Chilliwack, but never gone past there.

As we travel along, the driver points out the wild rhododendrons growing right beside the road. They're all woven in with the trees – it's an amazing sight, but things really change once we pass Hope. The mountains are awesome. They get higher and higher and the valley gets narrower and narrower until it almost feels like the peaks are going to close in on top of me. There's still snow on some of the highest parts of the mountains, but it's the Fraser Canyon that literally takes my breath away. The canyon walls go almost straight up and down in places and far below, the Fraser River shoots between them. Sometimes the road dips almost to the bottom of the canyon and from there I can see all the different layers of rocks that form the canyon walls. The range in colour is spectacular – browns, reds, yellows - you can almost see Picasso-like shapes in the rock walls.

When we come to Hell's Gate, I literally hang on to the edge of my seat. There's an aerial tram that crosses the river, taking tourists to the other side, giving them a too-close look at the rapids below and the huge, craggy boulders standing in the water. Even from this distance I can almost feel the force of the water pushing against those rocks. I can't imagine what it must be like in the tram, dangling above the river, trusting to a wire cable to keep you safe. For the first time, I have a real sense of the power of rushing water, and how it was able to carve out this canyon through all those layers of rock. It's pretty overwhelming, but I'm beginning to understand why tourists flock here. Fascinating as it is, it's frightening too. The driver stops the bus and we all get out to stretch out legs. When we climb back in, the driver smiles.

"Quite the view, isn't it?"

We nod in agreement, but I'm glad the bus is travelling on the right hand side of the road.

"Must be scary when you drive back down – I mean, you're so close to the edge," I say.

He laughs.

"Haven't gone over the side yet. There's guardrails – and it isn't really as close as it looks."

The doors swing shut with a pneumatic 'whoosh' and we're underway again.

Our next stop is Boston Bar. I welcome the chance to get out, stretch my legs and catch my breath. I'm still stunned by the power and violence of the river. The other passengers head into the coffee shop, and I join them. There's a lineup for the bathroom, and we chat, the way you talk with strangers, not really saying anything but just being friendly. Sahira doesn't come in with me. She says she doesn't want anything. I watched her for a minute, as she sat down on the bench outside the coffee shop, looking at the mountains like she was memorizing them. Then I go in, make my purchase and join her a few minutes later, holding two ice-cold bottles of water.

"Want one?" I ask, waving s bottle in her direction. She shakes her head and continues to stare at the mountains. We've still got a few hours of travel ahead of us, so I have a few sips of water, then stand up and stretch. I start to walk around the parking lot but I've hardly begun when the driver comes back out and tells everyone to re-board the bus.

"I'd like to come back and spend some time here," I tell Sahira, after we're back in our seats. "It's so different from Vancouver – wild, and almost overwhelming."

Sahira agrees. "Yes. Very nice."

I don't know what I expected – maybe talking over our future, or making plans, or something, but those are the only words Sahira speaks on the whole trip. The seat next to me might as well be vacant. She just sits there, turning Karli's teddy bear over and over in her hands, then hugging it to her. All I hear is a series of deep sighs. She doesn't even look out the window. I can't begin to imagine what's going on in her head.

Meanwhile, my own head is reeling. I'm excited about the job, looking forward to finding a place to live, and somehow, hoping to spend a little time writing. Maybe I should keep a journal while I'm out planting. Will there even be time? I truly don't know what to expect.

When we reach Kamloops, Anton's friend, Jeff, meets us at the depot.

"Welcome," he says, stretching out his arms for a big hug. "Anton's told me all about you."

I'm not sure if that's good or bad – but I'm not really paying attention to Jeff. I can't believe how hot it is. Hot and dry. I feel like I'm sitting in an oven – literally. When it gets warm at the coast, there's always an element of humidity. Here, it's just dry. The driest I've ever felt. I can feel my skin wrinkling already. It looks different, too. At the Coast, everything is green. All year round. I mean, sure there's snow sometimes, but everything is still green underneath it and there are always green trees. When you look at the mountains, you see green, except for the very top, where it's white in the wintertime. But here – there's almost nothing that's green. It's all shades of brown and tan and ochre and sand. It sort of goes with the heat – like the whole country has been popped in a toaster and come out brown. Even the river is more brown than green. It's going to take my eyes a while to get used to this.

The driver has opened the lift-up doors on the side of the bus, so we can get our luggage out.

"Let me give you a hand with your baggage," Jeff offers.

I shake my head. "That's okay. We've just got backpacks. We can handle them." I look over at the parking lot. "Which is your car?"

Jeff points to a shiny red Mustang convertible. It's a beauty. It's obviously been restored – and restored lovingly. And pampered after the restoration. I almost hesitate to put my grungy old backpack in the vehicle, but he swings open the trunk – the cleanest car trunk I've ever seen – and wedges our packs in firmly, so they won't slide around. Neat trick! I've never seen that done before. But then, I've never been this close to a restored Mustang convertible before, either.

"Fifteen minutes and you'll be home," Jeff announces. True to his word, we pull up at an apartment block almost to the minute, and follow him in.

"It's a two bedroom apartment," he explains. "You and Sahira can share the back bedroom – I was lucky to get a corner apartment, so we've got great ventilation."

I'm not sure why that's such a wonderful thing to have – I mean, it's nice to have good ventilation, but why is it so special?

He laughs at my puzzled expression. "We've got air conditioning of course – everyone does here, but I like it better with natural air unless it gets stupidly hot. Which it will, later in the summer. But with a corner apartment, you have windows on two walls, so you can almost always catch a bit of a breeze."

"You mean it gets hotter than this?"

"This is nothing. Wait until August."

I glance at Sahira. So far, she hasn't said a word to Jeff. Not even hello. It seems like it's going to take her a little while to get used to the idea of being away from home – and out from under her father's thumb. If it was me, I'd be dancing up and down and grinning from ear to ear, but it isn't me. She'll come to terms with things in her own way, I guess, and in her own time. At least, I hope she will. I'm already beginning to wonder if this was such a good idea.

"Dinner won't be for a while," Jeff says, glancing at his watch. "If you're like me, you'll want to get out and stretch your legs after spending all day sitting in the bus."

"Anyplace special we should go?" I ask.

"Nope. It's pretty hard to get lost around here. Just take your bearings from the mountains, and you'll be fine."

"I'll have to get my cell phone set up tomorrow," I tell him. "Dad warned me that using it on our server means everything is a long distance call."

He laughs. "Yep. I learned that the hard way. I'm off tomorrow, so I can take you around and help you get whatever errands done that you need."

I can see why Anton likes Jeff. He's one of the most positive, upbeat people I've ever met. Here we are, perfect strangers, and he's treating us like long-lost cousins or something. I'm glad of his offer – I'll need a day to get a bank account set up, shop for some work clothes and get a few other things done, so I can report for work as soon as possible. The money won't start coming in until I start shoving those trees in the ground.

"Anton should be here tomorrow," Jeff says. "He phoned last night to let me know what time he gets here."

"Too bad he couldn't come with us on the bus," I say.

"No way that would happen. Anton hates riding on the bus. He's flying up."

Good for him, I think, but flying costs more than riding a bus, so it isn't an option for me yet. Maybe someday. I wonder how he managed to convince his parents to spring for air fare, when they wanted him to stay and do summer courses. Must have been an interesting conversation! Then I try to imagine what the Fraser Canyon must look like from the air. Probably like something out of a National Geographic special.

"Come on, Sahira. Let's go exploring."

I expect her to respond to that – but she doesn't. Just shakes her head and hangs on to Karli's teddy bear.

Jeff looks at me and raises his eyebrows. I shrug my shoulders. It's like he's asking *"What's wrong with her?"* and I'm answering *"I don't know"*. He nods his head. I read that like *"Okay, let's just let her take her time."*

This guy is so cool. I've just met him, but it seems like I've known him forever. And we're able to communicate without words. That's super special.

I grin at Jeff, then head for the door. I'm anxious to have a look around and get my bearings. But most of all, I need to get out and walk. I can always think better when I'm walking, or running, or whatever. It's like moving my body gets my brain moving too. Right now, I've got a lot to think about, and part of it is wondering what's going on in Sahira's head, because it doesn't seem like she's really with me. Maybe it's just the shock of leaving home, or maybe it's something else. Whatever. For now, I'm just happy to be here.

CHAPTER TWELVE

"HEY, STUPID. WHADDA ya think you're doing?"

Ben's voice crackles with scorn.

"I'm digging a hole for my tree," I tell him, straightening up and leaning on my shovel.

"Yeah, well you're not digging a well," he retorts. "Look – this is how you do it."

Ben is my supervisor. Not like a boss or anything, but an experienced planter - someone who's done this many times before and can show me how it should be done. I guess, technically, he's my mentor. Or maybe my babysitter. I don't know if he gets paid extra for showing me the ropes. I hope so, because it's obvious he could plant a lot faster if he didn't have to look after me.

He takes his planting shovel, braces it against the ground and steps on it. Then he pries the shovel back, leaving a hole with a flap of earth above it, slips his shovel out and bends over to place a tree in the slit he's created. He holds the seeding with one hand while he replaces the flap, snuggling it around the seedling, then straightens up to step on the ground around it, stomping the dirt firmly into place.

"There. That's all you need – just a slit. But make it deep enough so the roots are straight."

He glares at me. "Okay? Try again."

I do, but the dirt where I'm working seems harder or denser or something, because my shovel doesn't slide in as easily as his did, and I have to lever it back and forth to get a slit wide enough to put the tree in. I drop to my knees, place the seedling, and pat the earth around it, with my hands.

"Oh, Jeez," he sputters. "What the fuck do you think you're doing now?"

He isn't interested in an explanation and cuts me off when I begin to explain.

"Look. You bend over at the waist. And you stomp the dirt back. You can't pat it in place like you're patting cookies into shape. You have to stomp it, or the seedling is going to flop over and probably die. And you don't want to kneel down like that every time you put a seedling in the ground. By noon you won't be able to walk because you're lifting your bag of seedlings every time you stand up and your quads will give out before you know it. Just bend from the waist and save yourself a lot of work. And if you step the dirt back in place, it's firmer than patting it with your dainty little hands."

Shit. He doesn't have to be sarcastic. For some reason, he's really annoyed that I'm patting the dirt into place. I've never done this before and I'm trying my best, but he obviously wishes he was somewhere else – or that I'd been given to someone else to train. I move over a little way and try again. I dig my shovel in, ready to make a slit the way he showed me, but that generates another bellow.

"Jeez, don't you know anything? The seedlings have to be seven feet apart. That's not seven feet. Plant them as close as you're doing, and they won't have room enough to grow."

I bite my tongue, move further away and try to eyeball seven feet.

"Here," he says, lifting his shovel. "This is about four feet long. A little less than two shovel lengths is about perfect.

"Don't worry. You'll catch on once you've measured it a few times. Do another one."

Then he smiles. He smiles! He might be human after all.

That was only the beginning of my day. If I'd ever thought tree planting was glamorous, I now know better. I didn't expect the long days or the constant activity. It seems like we're always working – picking up our trees, packing them to our assigned area, digging them in, picking up more trees, walking to the next site, then repeating the whole process. Again. And again. And it's backbreaking work. I didn't know I could get this tired, and still keep moving.

I know we were lucky to get taken on – some of the crews started in April and pretty well all of them got out in the field sometime in May. That's why most tree planters are university students – it fits in timewise with their summer vacations. But some people just can't take it. The work is too hard, they aren't prepared for the living conditions, they don't have a clear idea of what they're getting into – or they injure themselves. That's what happened on our crew. Two people dropped out (we never learned why) so there were a couple of vacancies to fill.

"Don't think of them as trees," one of the other planters tells me, as we drive out to the work site. "Think of dropping quarters into the ground."

We're paid on a per-tree basis. You get eight cents for some trees, twenty-five cents for others. That seemed pretty strange when I first heard about it – I mean, a tree is a tree, right? So why is one more valuable than another? I soon learned it depends on the territory. Some tree lots offer easy planting and others are real bitches. Hillsides. Rocky terrain. Swampy ground. Places where thinning crews have cleared out thick underbrush so a tree can go in, but there's scrub lying around, roots in the ground that make digging hard, and other shit to contend with. There are lots of things that make planting in one site easier than in another. Experienced planters snap up the good sites, leaving us ignorant rookies to work on the crappiest sites. Instead of dropping quarters into the ground, it's more like I'm dropping dimes.

Aside from the hard work, there are things I can't control. Like the bugs. I slather myself with repellant before leaving camp, to protect me from the bugs. That works for about the first 15 minutes. Then I start to sweat and the repellant washes off and runs into my eyes. Or maybe it's just the sweat. Whatever, my eyes start to sting, then the tears begin to flow and snot drips from my nose. I'm an itchy mess all over. I can't even imagine what Tiffany would say if she could see me now.

The planting crews usually go through a training session at the beginning of the season, but we missed that, so me and Anton each got assigned to tag along with one of the experienced planters. My guy is Ben, Anton's is Liz. I think Anton got the best of the deal – Liz doesn't bellow at him, and she's not sarcastic. I hear a lot of laughter over where they are, and wonder if I can change instructors.

This morning felt like the first day of school – new, exciting and upbeat. The start of an adventure! I thought it would be easy to plant trees – you just dig a hole and drop a seedling into it. Right? Wrong! You have to pick the right place for a seedling – not just the right distance away from other seedlings, but you have to check for boulders, other trees, run-off channels – there are dozens of things that dictate where you put that precious seedling. I learn each part of the process the hard way, with a solid accompaniment of wheezes and grunts from Ben. There's a noise he makes each time I goof. It's sort of 'Oh, shit, what did I do to deserve this' all compressed into a giant exhalation, while his lips sort of rumble back and forth and he makes a snorting noise, like a horse. I don't know if he rolls his eyes or not, but it feels like it. I hear that noise lots of times during that first morning. Even for stuff like drinking water –"You gotta drink more or you're gonna get sick" Ben growls – or eating snacks "You gotta keep eating or you'll run out of steam. And I ain't gonna pack you outta here."

After one of the longest mornings on record, it's time for our lunch break and we find a dry log to sit on while we unwrap the lunches we'd made that morning. My lettuce and tomato sandwiches are now a soggy mess. I look at Ben's lunch. Peanut butter and something that looks like a layer of chocolate.

I point to his sandwich. "Peanut butter and chocolate?"

"Nutella," he smiles. "Ever tried it?"

I shake my head.

"Great stuff. Hazelnuts and chocolate. Goes good with peanut butter. Lots of calories – so that means lots of energy. And it tastes good."

He wolfs down two of the sandwiches, chomping away happily, then cracks open a hard-boiled egg. After that, he unwraps a granola bar. I look at it longingly. My chocolate chip cookies are a dismal pile of crumbs. I eat them anyway. He finishes off with an apple. My banana is almost inedible. It's mashed out of shape, brown and squishy. So much for the most disastrous lunch ever. Ben doesn't say anything about it – he doesn't have to. But I'll know better tomorrow. Too soon, it's time to get back on the job.

I pick up a new tray of seedlings and transfer them to my planting bag. Before I can take three steps, I hear Ben holler.

"Where's your sticker?"

"What sticker?" He makes 'that' noise again.

"That sticker on the end of the seedling tray. Take it off of each tray when you unload it, and put it somewhere safe. You have to give them to the camp manager at the end of each shift. That's how they know how many trees you've planted – and how much to pay you."

That makes sense. No one is going to stand on site and count every tree as I plant it. I go back to the pile of trays, loosen the sticker from the trays I've already planted, add my new sticker to the pile, and bury them all in the back pocket of my jeans.

The afternoon drags on. I'm beginning to realize that my dream of financial independence isn't going to happen this summer – not at the rate I'm planting. I know I'm slowing down, but the ground gets harder and harder. I think again about the ads that offered 'up to $15,000 per season' and realize that I'm going to be in the 'up to' category. Pretty close to the bottom of the category. At this rate, I'll be lucky to make enough for the bus fare home.

I hack away at the ground again, until Ben reaches into his pack and hands me a file. I look at it blankly. I don't know what he wants me to do with it.

Another of 'those' sighs.

"Sharpen the edge of your blade. Goes in a lot better."

I rasp at the edge of the shovel and try again. He's right. It is easier. The afternoon wears on. I can see the angle of the sun changing, and shadows moving slowly across the ground, but I've lost all track of time and I'm too tired to look at my watch. I hurt. Everywhere. And every square inch of exposed skin has been bitten by something. It's beyond itching. What isn't aching or itching is sunburned. I'm ready to cry, but I damn well refuse. Ben's so bloody sarcastic I know he'd laugh his stupid head off if I did.

I'm surprised when he walks toward me. "Come on. Time to head back to the truck. We're done for the day."

He gives me a hug, and laughs. "Hey – you did pretty good for your first day."

Then I do cry. Ben pretends he doesn't see the tears trickle down my cheeks, cutting a path through the grime and guck.

"Let's go."

We walk back to the pickup site, load our empty boxes into the truck, climb aboard and rumble back to camp. I stagger into my tent and crash, without even taking my boots off. It seems like seconds later that Anton's rattling the fly on my tent.

"Come on. Dinner's ready."

"Go away."

"No – you've got to eat."

"I'm too tired."

"Christie, come out of there. Now." Then he makes a sing-songy voice. "I'll huff and I'll puff and I'll blow your tent down."

I can't help but laugh.

"How come you're not tired?" I whine, crawling out.

"I am – but I know we have to eat or we'll be really bagged tomorrow."

I don't know what I expected. Maybe not something quite as simple as hot dogs over a campfire, but I'm surprised at what we do get. The cook shack is set up like a buffet and there's lots of food. The cooks stand behind two tubs of chili – one with meat and the other vegetarian. Crusty buns and tubs of salad are next in line, and then there's a desert table loaded with pies, fresh fruit and even ice cream. I didn't know how hungry I was until I start loading my plate.

While we're eating, I look around at some of the other planters. Some of them have so many scabs on their faces they look like something out of a horror movie, but when I make a comment to the guy sitting across from me, he says they'll turn human again in the fall, once the planting season is over. "By that time, we'll have so much money it won't matter what we look like." He laughs at his own joke.

During dinner, we categorize the bugs we've met so far: biting flies that include no-see-ums, deer flies, horse flies, black flies and sand flies. Mosquitoes are a given. And one of the guys had the bad luck to run into a wasp nest so he's got some truly impressive bumps.

"Don't forget the ticks," someone calls. Great. I think about the horror stories I've heard about people getting weird diseases from ticks. And you can't even see them! They get under your clothes and dig in. It's a pretty gross topic for the dinner table, but everyone wades in with their own horror stories.

After dinner, some of the planters stay in the cook shack to read, while others gather around a campfire. I spot a couple of guitars and a harmonica. Looks like fun, but I'm too tired to join in tonight. Maybe another night. I head back to my tent and crawl in. I'm really glad we have single tents so I can spread my stuff out and just relax. After about ten seconds of relaxing, I'm sound asleep and don't hear anything until the cook clatters an iron triangle, calling everyone in for breakfast the next morning.

I'm not sure I can even get out of my tent, never mind walk to the cook shack or go to work, but Anton's there to pry me out again. Everything hurts – my back, my legs, my hands – everything. I hobble over to the cook shack, where mugs of coffee, stacks of pancakes, scrambled eggs, hash browns and crisp bacon help make the trip worthwhile. Then we make up our lunches head out to the truck. Anton and I stand together, waiting for the driver to appear.

Seconds later, my mentor walks up, a big smile on his face. "How ya' doin'?"

"Okay, I guess."

"Little stiff?"

"LOT stiff."

"Thought so." Then he sighs. "I sure wish you'd been here for orientation." He plants himself in front of me and Anton.

"Two things you gotta do. After you get back to camp, you stretch. Complete body stretches." He looks at us. "Either of you know yoga?" When we shake our heads he nods, as if confirming what he already knew. "I'll show you some later.

"The second thing is, you gotta stretch first thing in the morning too. We can do that now."

The other planters grin. I saw a couple of them stretching back at camp, but I never thought about joining them. At this point I don't care how funny I look so I follow Ben's lead. It hurts at first, but it helps and before it's time to climb aboard the truck, I'm moving more freely. Who'd have thought someone like Ben would be into yoga?

"Something else you'll need to watch for," he says, as we unload our gear at the drop site. "That's tendonitis." My blank look clues him in that I don't have any idea what tendonitis is. "It usually hits your wrists – and it's something that almost every planter gets. It's really important to warm up before you start planting. Squeeze something in your hand, nice and gentle, just to get those tendons working.

"Once they're warmed up, put your fist against a wall, a tree – anything immovable, and push against it. Hard. Then relax. Do that a couple of dozen times. And once you get to the planting block – start slow. Even if you have creamy ground, start slow to warm up your body."

Creamy ground? I don't want to look stupid and ask what that is, but I guess he already knows how dumb I am.

"Creamy ground is nice dirt. No rocks, roots, stumps – the stuff where seedlings almost plant themselves. One other thing you should do is learn to plant with both hands. We usually do the first and last bundle of each bag with our other hand."

Now I know he's pulling my leg. I start to laugh – but he's serious. "It makes a difference. Trust me. I know." He turns to Anton. "I guess you don't have any ice packs, do you?"

Anton stutters – "Uh, no, we don't."

"When you get your days off, pick up a couple of the blue gel packs and keep them in the freezer. There's a special one in the cook shack, so you don't mix your stuff up with the food. Meantime, remember that creek behind the cook shack? If your wrists start to swell, sink them into the creek. It's not ice water, but it's pretty cold. It'll help."

I start to point out that our wrists aren't swollen, but he's already turned away. Too soon we're back to business, strapping on our bags and loading in the bundles. I waddle over to Ben but he waves me off.

"You're on your own today. Have a good one - I'll see you on the lunch break."

He gives a two finger salute and strides off, looking relaxed, rested and ready to go.

Anton shrugs, and we look around, picking the spot where we'll start our day's work.

It's the first day on my own and it's one of the hardest days of my life. If I thought yesterday was a pain, today is even worse. It will take another day or so before I get into the rhythm of planting, learn to move at a steady pace, conserve energy, and remember to take regular breaks. Ben was right. Those breaks are really important – so I rehydrate, eat some fruit or a granola bar, and do some stretches, to keep my muscles limber. And drink some water. Not just polite little sips, but great long gulps. I can't believe how thirsty I get.

The days follow, one after another, like the endless stream of seedlings I'm planting. I don't know what day it is, and I don't even care anymore. We're up at first light, dress quickly and head to the cook shack for breakfast (mine is getting bigger and bigger – Tiffany would have a fit if she knew how many calories I'm consuming). After breakfast, I make up my lunch and my snacks, replenish my water bottles, and head over to the truck. We load all our stuff in the back, then head for the bench seats in the cab of the truck, to lurch and grind our way out to the site, like a bunch of robots. No one's talking or laughing. It's like that Disney movie Fantasia I saw when I was a kid. I've never forgotten that sequence where the figures just keep going and going and going, like some kind of machine. That's us. We'll just keep planting and planting and planting forever.

But suddenly, it's the end of our rotation. Every 12 days, the crews get a break and head back into town, while one of the 'floating' crews takes over. We have two glorious days to sleep in, soak in a hot tub, wash our clothes, and replenish our supplies. I'm looking forward to seeing my new digs. While Anton and I were out planting, Sahira was supposed to find a place for the two of us to stay. It was good of Jeff to let us bunk in till we get settled somewhere, but it wasn't intended to be a permanent arrangement. Anton is staying with Jeff for the summer though, and heading back to Vancouver when university starts. Me and Sahira will stay in Kamloops, in our own apartment, while she goes to TRU and I work on my book. I'm excited about us having a place of our own and wonder if we'll be able to move right in or if we have to wait until the end of the month. And I wonder if we'll be lucky enough to have cross ventilation, like Jeff has.

As it turns out, the right answer is (c) – none of the above. Sahira isn't there.

Jeff hands me an envelope. "She left this for you," he says. "Sorry, but there wasn't any way to get hold of you."

It's short and simple.

Christie: Sorry, but I can't stay here. I don't feel comfortable staying with a strange man, even if he isn't really a man. Not really a man? Oh, shit. She's talking about Jeff being gay. That's funny. Of all the things she might have to worry about, a gay guy is the last one to cause problems of *'that'* kind. But it isn't really funny. I didn't know she felt that way about gays. Not that we've ever talked about it. I stop my train of thought for a minute. Yeah, like there's so *many* things we've never talked about. But this one really surprises me - especially when Anton has been so helpful and Jeff has been so generous. The note continues.

My father would kill me if he found out. I shake my head. There she goes, exaggerating again. *I got student housing at TRU. I know it's not what we planned, but I don't want to keep riding the bus all the time, and it's easier just to stay on campus. Hope you can find a place okay.*

Sahira.

PS – How's the planting going? Must be fun being out in the woods.

And that's it. All our plans out the window. That last comment really pisses me off. How's the planting going? As if she cared. As if she had even the smallest idea of what it was all about. How hard it was. Fun? When every muscle in my body aches? Fun? Sleeping on the ground in a pup tent? Fun? No hot showers, no TV, no anything except what you can pack in by yourself.

I look again at the note. She doesn't give a phone number, or a room number, or any way to get in touch with her. It's probably just an oversight. At least I hope so. But the bottom line is, I'm on my own. And staying in Kamloops by myself for the winter isn't what I'd envisioned.

Anton's eyebrows ask a question. I smile back. "She's staying on campus. Makes life easier."

He isn't buying it, but I'm not going into it right now. It's Jeff who asks the question: "You still want to stay here?"

"If you'll have me."

He grins. "Any time. Any friend of Anton's is a friend of mine. Now – let's eat."

One of the pluses of staying with Jeff, is that he's a great cook. We start off with a salad unlike any I've ever had: tiny sweet, red cherry tomatoes, strips of golden yellow peppers, and green grapes. In our house, salad was always a shredded lettuce leaf, a sliced tomato and some cucumber. Once in a while, dad would buy some potato salad at the deli, but that was the extent of it. What Jeff's given us is exciting to the eye, and lights up my whole mouth. A wonderful mixture of flavours and textures.

"Any way we can convince you to come out and be our camp cook?" Anton laughs.

Jeff shakes his head. "Not at the moment. I'm too busy with the job I've got." Jeff's started an apprenticeship, learning to be an electrician.

Somehow, the two days slip by, with still a dozen things left to do. They'll have to wait until next time. There's no laundromat at the campsite, so last time I pretty much lived in my clothes. This time I've got clean stuff to change into after work, extra socks and underwear, and a few other things that I really missed on the last rotation. I even bought a book about yoga. Anton laughed when he saw it, but he and Jeff joined me in trying out a few positions. They're weird. I mean, you move body parts in different ways and some of them are pretty much impossible, but others feel really good. Some of the names are hilarious. Downward Facing Dog. I guess in a way, the pose does look like that, but I crack up every time I do it. The Chair is another one – hands stretched out in front of you, like you were reaching for something to hang onto, and your bum sticking out back, like you're going to ease down into a chair. There's several more, but once I start doing them, they feel surprisingly good – and surprisingly challenging. The Plank looks like the easiest one – just balance down on the ground, on your forearms and your toes, with your body held straight inbetween. Nothing to it. Ha! Within ten seconds my trunk is quivering and threatening to collapse. I can see I've got a lot to work on.

My last purchase is a blank journal. If I'm going to write, I'll need something to write in – and I can't bring my laptop out to the campsite. I even have the germ of an idea for a story. It's sort of fantasy – about someone who gets trapped in Facebook. Like they suddenly become their image and swoop into the world behind their computer screen. They can only interact with people who are already on Facebook, but in order to break free, they have to find a way to contact someone who's still outside. I haven't figured out how it's all going to happen, but it'll be something to think about while I'm stuffing those trees in the ground.

CHAPTER THIRTEEN

THE FIRST DAY back is awful. All my muscles seem to have vanished, and it's like I'm starting right from the beginning, but this time I remember what Ben told me and do some stretching during the day, and more when we get back to camp. I'm not quite as dead tired at the end of the shift, so I stay up for a while after dinner, getting to know some of the other kids. Well, they aren't all kids. There's a couple of really old people in the crew – they're probably 40 or so – and I can't imagine why they're doing this.

When I point them out to Anton, he starts to laugh. "I know that pair – we talked before. I'll tell you later. Right now, let's go get some food."

The meals here are amazing. I don't know how the cooks do what they do, given the conditions they're working under, but they're definitely a hazard to my waistline. Good solid main courses, with awesome deserts. And snacks. Lots of snacks. Delicious snacks. I tell myself I'm burning off thousands of calories every day, but I know I'm kidding myself. Now I know how bears must feel, fattening up for the winter. But I'm not quite ready to hibernate yet.

After dinner, I think about that blank journal I bought, crawl into my tent and rummage in my pack. There it is, tucked away in a plastic bag, waiting for me, like a new friend. We'll have lots to learn about each other, and now is as good a time as any to begin. It looks quite pretty, actually – with embossed covers that look a bit like leather but aren't, a red spine and red triangles on the corners. It even has a black cord ending in a tassel, to use as a bookmark.

I thought that was something they only did back in the olden days, but here it is, and it's going to come in handy. I always lose bookmarks, but this one won't wander off. I scratch the bar code sticker off the back and enjoy the feel of the book in my hand.

Okay. Time to open it and quit stalling. I admire the pages, run my finger around the edges and skim my fingertips across the pages, barely touching them. I can almost feel the words I'm going to sprinkle on them. They'll be pure magic, almost like star dust. I pick up my pen, roll it in my fingers and click the ballpoint in and out. So now what? The page is waiting, the pen is ready – all that isn't in gear is my brain. What do I write in a journal anyway? Write about my day? I planted a tree. I planted another tree. Then I planted another tree. That doesn't make exciting reading – or spark any great thoughts in my brain.

I look at the page again. Is it a trick of light, or is that a disembodied laugh floating across it? It's neither. My tent fly rattles, and a familiar voice interrupts.

"Hey, Christie. Come on out."

It's Anton – and he's brought a couple of friends.

"We're gonna walk up to the waterfall. Want to come?"

Waterfall? Who knew? "Sure. Be right out."

I put the journal back in my pack, tuck the pen beside it and crawl out of the tent. Maybe a description of the waterfall will make a good first entry into the journal. A voice in the back of my head says, "Really? Is that how great authors work? Goofing off at every opportunity?"

Oh, knock it off, I tell the voice. *I need to have something to write about. And I need to meet some of the people here in camp.*

"This is Mark, and this is Donna," Anton says. "This is their third year planting."

"Wow! That's impressive."

"Not really," Donna smiles. "It was either this or end up with humungous student loans."

Mark chimes in. "Yep. Besides, it's so much fun." We all laugh at that. "Come on – we don't want to lose the light."

The long evenings mean there's time to do stuff after dinner - lots of time. I'm surprised the camp manager doesn't send everyone out for a couple more hours of planting, but people seem to find things to do. As soon as dusk comes, they head for their tents. The evenings may be long but the mornings come early. Very early.

I follow along as Mark and Donna head up a little canyon. Part way along, Donna calls back, "I guess we should have told you to bring a camera."

"I don't have one. Didn't think I'd need it."

"Well, you can always come back later."

I did bring my cell phone, so I can take pictures with that.

When we reach the waterfall, it's not quite what I expected. I guess I'd been thinking about Niagara Falls or something, with a huge pillow of water billowing over a cliff, and a curtain of water screening the rock face. This is more of a trickle than a curtain, and it sort of oozes out from the cliff, gathers itself together part way down and turns into a mini-fall. In its own way, it's really pretty. Lots of ferns and mosses grow around it, and there's a little pool at the bottom with what appear to be little fish in it. How can that be? There's no way fish could be in a place like that.

Mark laughs at the surprised look on my face.

"Yeah – it's amazing, isn't it?"

I have to ask. "Are those really fish?"

"Fish? Here? Come on Christie." Anton makes a face. "We're a long way from the ocean."

"Take a look," I tell him.

He spots the little wriggling bodies in the water. "Hey- they are!"

"No, they aren't," Mark says. "They're salamanders - something like lizards. They lay eggs near a source of water, and when the young hatch out, they're amphibious. When they're fully grown, they leave the water and return to the land."

"I thought salamanders lived in the tropics or someplace like that," Anton says. "For sure not in Kamloops!"

Mark shakes his head. "Actually, there are more than 100 different kinds, and they go from about the length of your thumbnail to almost as long as your arm."

"But the big ones don't live here," Donna chimes in. "Just the little guys."

"So are you guys biologists or something?"

Donna laughs. "Nope – not even naturalists. Sometimes we see stuff when we're out here and when we get home again, we look it up on the internet, to find out more about it." She points to some of the mosses surrounding the pond. "I love these tiny flowers."

I have to look closely to see them, but there they are: miniature dots of red against the green moss. Who knew? When you look closely, there's lots of see. Lots of stuff that this city gal has never noticed before.

"Time to head back," Mark announces. He's right. Somehow, the sun has slipped below the horizon and we're into the twilight hour.

Back at camp, we head for our tents. There's another long day coming up tomorrow. I'll definitely write about the mosses and the salamanders – not tonight, because it's not light enough in the tent, but definitely tomorrow.

This rotation is easier and seems to go quicker. I'm planting more efficiently. I have my own file, to keep my spade sharp. And, despite how clumsy it feels,

I've learned to plant with both hands. In spite of that, Anton and I both end up with red, swollen wrists. Lucky Ben told us about the blue gel packs – and now's the time to haul them out and get the swelling under control.

I finally meet up with the older couple Anton mentioned and they turn out to be really interesting. When I ask what they do the rest of the year, they laugh. It seems they have a place down in Mexico and that's where they go every winter. "We can make enough planting to live like kings down there," he says. "Well, maybe not kings," his wife adds, "but pretty high up on the scale."

Some of the other planters are really interesting too. They come from all across Canada and all walks of life. That's a corny phrase, but it really fits here. One of the guys used to be top ranked in the planting field – he was the one who earned fantastic amounts of money every year and it sounded like his seedlings almost flew into the ground by themselves.

"He held top spot for eleven years," Mike tells me, "but last year he got tendonitis really bad, right at the beginning of the season."

"What happened then?"

"They give you a choice," Mike explains. "You can either leave the camp, or you can get reassigned to what they euphemistically call alternate chores. Doesn't pay as much, but it's better than nothing."

I find out later that 'alternate chores' are another way of saying 'scut work' around the camp. Ben says it's a euphuism for cleaning latrines, looking after garbage, loading seedlings into trays. If you can handle it, you might be sent out to de-limb the jack pines – clearing away the dead lower limbs so planters can move around easier. It helps reduce the fire danger too. I'd never thought about it before, but fire is a very real danger out in the woods - especially in August, when things are literally tinder dry. Ben tells me that sometimes they have to close the forests and prohibit anyone – including planters - from entering, because the trees and the underbrush gets into a really dangerous condition called pyrogenesis.

"Called what?"

He smirks. I've discovered he loves using big words, or technical terms. Or maybe he just loves proving how smart he is, by explaining the big words to people like me. "Pyrogenesis is when things heat up enough to combust spontaneously."

Wow! Spontaneous combustion, euphuism, pyrogenesis. Dad would laugh if he heard this conversation. He's a scrabble nut and loves finding mega-tile words to tag onto existing ones and rack up a ba-jillion points. We used to play a lot of scrabble together – some of my spelling wasn't so good, but Dad pretended to find the words in the dictionary – just the way I'd spelled them. Later, when my spelling improved, I looked for a few of those words and discovered they'd never existed. But that's the kind of dad he was.

At the end of the rotation, I head back to Kamloops with a long list of stuff that will hopefully get done in my two days off.

There's another letter from Sahira waiting for me at Jeff's place.

> *Sorry, but I don't have a phone. Can I see you next time you're in town? There's a phone in the office that we can use during office hours, or you can leave a message there. I really miss my cell and my computer. I have to do homework in the library. They have computers there but you have to sign up ahead of time to use them. That scholarship looked huge, but it just covers the essentials. I'll have to look for a part-time job if I want any extras. Need anyone else on the planting crew?*
>
> *Hugs*
> *Sahira*

At the bottom of the letter, she's written in the office phone number and the hours when the office is open. Of course, it's closed on the weekend so there's no one there now. Just a recorded message inviting me to leave a message after the tone. I hate those things, but when the beep sounds, I tell the machine this is a message for someone in the student residence and before I can even begin the message, it beeps again and a voice that sounds like it was computer generated, thanks me for leaving the message. I all but scream at it. "I haven't left a message yet, you dumb fucking machine". I take a couple of deep breaths and dial again – then realize it's going to be easier if I write out what I need to say and just read it off.

'This is a message for Sahira Grewal, in student residence'. I give Jeff's landline number, and tell her I know she probably won't get the message until... I was going to say until Monday, because the office is closed, when the machine cuts me off again. Shit. I try again, and this time just give her name and Jeff's phone number, and say I'll call her the next time I'm in town. It's hard to believe that more than a month has gone by without us seeing each other. It's probably the first time in our lives that we haven't been together at least once a day, and once we got our phones, we texted back and forth ten times a day. Now I can't talk to her, can't text her, can't even write her a letter because I don't know the residence address or her room number. It's totally frustrating. We'll have to figure out a better system than this.

Nothing is working out the way I thought it would. I'd planned to give Dad his cheque back at the end of the season, but I need money now, so I cashed it and started a bank account. Once upon a time I thought I could make enough at tree-planting to be independent, and pay my own way. Not just for the summer, but after that as well, so I could concentrate on writing and not have to get a part time job or anything. It's obvious that's not going to happen, partly because Anton and I started late, but mostly because I'm not a very fast planter.

Maybe I should move someplace where it doesn't cost much to live, like those guys with their place in Mexico, and I could write my book there. Yeah. In my dreams. Still, it would be fun to think about. Anyway, I'm going to need an allowance if I stay here for the winter. That's something I'll have to decide when the season ends. Do I want to stay in Kamloops by myself? Jeff said I could stay in his place, but I don't know if I want to do that. On the other hand, getting an apartment by myself might be too expensive. Do I want to go home, and cope with Tiffany again? It would be cheaper, but I'm not sure I could put up with her all day every day. At least when I was going to school I got a break away from her during the day. And then there's Karli. How much work would I actually be able to do? Realistically, I know there would be lots of interruptions. There's a lot to think about, and it's lucky I don't have to decide right now. All I have to do is get through a couple more rotations. Since Anton and I started so late, our 'season' is only going to be seven rotations – and we're already going into the third one. It's weird to think I'm almost half way through the planting season.

The journal still sits in the bottom of my backpack – nice and clean and empty, just like the day I bought it. Somehow, I never had the time or energy to write in it last rotation, but I promise myself to do better this time and write something every day.

Once again the days off are over before everything is done. We get back to camp late and don't see anyone. Next morning, everyone is buzzing at breakfast. One of the guys read something in the paper about a father beheading four of his kids. Ungh. I just about heaved when I heard it. He was determined to share all the gory details with everyone and said it was an 'honour killing'. I didn't think that still happened, but another of the guys said it really did, and told us about a neighbor of his who got sent to prison for killing his sister a couple of years ago. According to Jimmy, Waqus Parvez, strangled his sixteen-year old sister.

"You mean, he just got mad at her and strangled her?" Anton asks.

"No – he wasn't mad at her. It was an honour killing. His father told him to do it."

Kill someone when you aren't even mad at them? That's hard to believe, and I say so.

Jimmy looks at me and shakes his head. "It happens. World wide, a couple of thousand women die each year, in honour killings"

That blows my mind. "A couple of thousand? How come you never hear about it?

"Sometimes you do," he says.

"But why?"

"Mostly because a girl does something her family doesn't approve of. Marries someone without permission. Or elopes. Or has a boyfriend. It's different for you. You can go out with a guy, or be friends with him, but in some cultures, that dishonours the family, and there's only one way to wipe out the stain. It's pretty hard on girls from other cultures who move here, because they just want to do what their friends at school are doing."

Well, sure. Hanging out, dating, that's just part of being a teenager.

"It happens mostly in India or Asia," he says, "but it happens in Canada too – there's been at least half a dozen cases in the last few years."

Sahira's words come back to me. *My father would kill me if he knew.* I'd laughed it off as an exaggeration, but now it sends a shiver down my spine. Would he? What if it was true? Have I unknowingly put her life in danger? It's a scary thought – but not as scary as the one that follows it. The bruises on Sahira's back. And the way she wears long sleeves, even on the hottest days. What has she been covering up? And why haven't I noticed anything before? This is my best friend – we've grown up together, and I thought I knew everything about her. My mind skitters around, like walking over a frozen puddle, waiting for the surface to break. It can't be what I'm thinking, can it?

Everyone is real quiet after that, and when we load into the trucks and head out to our plots, it's like someone has turned down the volume on the whole camp. No one is joking or kidding around, like they usually do. Suddenly, the whole thing is too close to home. I tell myself that not all South Asian parents are like that – that the majority are loving and caring and would never think of such a thing. But Sahira herself believed that her father might – no, that couldn't be right. But then why did she say it? And why did I brush it away so lightly. How stupid could I be? How blind? Now I have to wonder, just how safe is Sahira? And what can I do to help her? There's no way to contact her until my next leave, and that's a week and a half away. It seems like a year and a half.

I don't know who I'm speaking to, but I send a fervent prayer to Whoever is there, that Sahira will be safe.

CHAPTER FOURTEEN

THE RIDE BACK seems to last forever, but once we get back to camp, I grab Anton.

"We have to talk."

"Sure. What's up?"

"I'm scared for Sahira. How safe is she going to be in residence?"

"Pretty safe, I'd guess. Why?"

"I was thinking about those honour killings."

"Oh, come on," he says. "Sahira's dad isn't like that."

"I didn't used to think so either," I admit. "But lately, I've been thinking about some of the things she's said – and different things that happened. Or didn't happen."

He looks puzzled. "Didn't happen?"

"I mean things that she wasn't allowed to do. I never thought much of it at the time, but when you put them all together, it starts to add up to something pretty ugly."

"Just because her dad is strict . . ."

"It's more than that. He hates her. I thought she was exaggerating, but if she's told me once, she's told me dozens of times, that her dad hates her – that he's always hated her because she wasn't a boy."

Anton starts to laugh. "Would help if we told him it was his fault? Sperm decides the sex – so he's the one who made a girl."

"It's nothing to laugh at," I say. "He'd never believe you, in any case. His mind was made up right from the day she was born – and nothing is going to change it. It might have been different if Sahira's mom had other kids, but she didn't. I never knew all that stuff about honour killings before, but it scares me, and I don't know what to do."

Anton's smile vanishes. "I never knew Sahira's dad felt that way."

"Well, she probably didn't tell everyone. How hard would be it be to say 'My Dad hates me'? She's told me, because we've been best friends forever, but it would be pretty hard to say that to someone you didn't really know – or couldn't really trust. I don't think I could tell anyone if my dad was like that." I pause. How much should I tell him?

"There's something else – he beats up on her. I've seen scars on her back and bruises, lots of times. She keeps saying she's been clumsy and fallen on the stairs or something – but you know, and I know, that clumsy isn't a word you'd ever use with Sahira."

He's quiet for a few minutes, thinking that over.

"How about her mom? She must know if her dad's doing that."

"Sahira never says much about her mom. And in all the years I've known her, I don't think Sahira's mom has said much more than 'hello' to me. She's friendly enough, but it isn't like we're chums or anything." I laugh. "Now that I think of it, I'm not even sure she speaks English."

"She has to," Anton says, but there's a pause before he adds, "Doesn't she?"

"Why? She never goes anywhere without Sahira's dad. She shops at those East Indian stores on Main Street, and she only gets what he tells her to. My guess? She feels guilty because Sahira is a girl, and she couldn't produce a son. And maybe being beaten was how she was brought up. I don't know."

Anton shakes his head. He's bewildered. "This sounds like something out of the middle ages."

I can only agree with him. "That's what I thought too – but I'm not making this up. If I was, it would have a happier ending than this. The thing that really pisses me off is, I thought I was helping Sahira by telling her not to get married, and encouraging her to run away. Now it sounds like I might have been putting her in serious danger. I can't believe how stupid I've been."

We look at each other, but there's a big blank between us. I don't think Anton quite believes me. It's hard to wrap your mind around something so weird.

"Anyway, "I continue, "I hope Sahira leaves her phone number with Jeff so we can make contact. I don't even know where she's staying – just somewhere in residence."

"Couldn't you send her an email?" Anton suggests

Stupid, stupid, stupid. I slap my forehead. Berating myself doesn't do any good, but that's such a simple solution I can't believe I didn't think of it weeks ago. I know she doesn't have her own computer, but she uses the university's computers in the library, so yes, of course she can get emails.

"If there's no message at Jeff's, I'll use his computer and set something up."

The days crawl by, like snails oozing through dead pine needles. I feel like some kind of robot working solely by rote: lift a seedling, slice a hole, drop it in, tramp it down, pick up another – an endless, meaningless cycle. When we first started planting, I was excited about the role I was playing, helping the forest to grow again, restoring nature, and all that other good stuff. Yeah. What a laugh. Like I'm some sort of Wonder Woman, making great things happen, all by herself. Oh – and then there are those magic bracelets. Maybe that's where it all went wrong. I don't have any magic bracelets. If I'd only eaten a few more boxes of cereal, I could have sent the box tops in to get my very own magic bracelet. Well, okay. That's pretty sick because there's really nothing funny about this situation, but every time I try to think it through, I come up against a blank wall.

The question that keeps circling around in my brain, is, does Sahira know she's in danger? Or does she think everything is okay because I told her it was. Shit. I jam my shovel into the ground and realize I've cut a seedling in half. I bury it, fast, before anyone sees, and plant another in that space. Now I can't even plant a tree, without screwing things up.

Eventually, our rotation ends. It takes seconds to dash to my tent, scoop up my bag and hop on the back of the truck heading into town. Anton's right behind me.

I hardly stop to say 'Hi' to Jeff, before I check the mail. Nothing from Sahira, but there's a letter from my dad. I'll read it later. "Any messages?" I ask him.

He shakes his head.

"Okay if I use your computer?"

"Sure. Go ahead."

I tap out a quick message to Sahira. At least Yahoo doesn't let me down. Now it's just a question of waiting for her to respond, and I cross my fingers that she'll check her mail quickly. Meanwhile, I fill Jeff in on what's happening.

He's as gob-smacked as I was. "You're shitting me."

"Nope. Now we have to figure out what to do to protect Sahira."

We look at each other, then Anton turns to me.

"No brilliant ideas?"

"I've given up on brilliant ideas," I say. "It was my brilliant idea that created this mess. I thought about going to the police, but what do I tell them? My friend might be in danger? They'd laugh at me. I don't have any proof of any of this."

Anton agrees, but Jeff's got something else in mind.

"How good are the odds that her dad will find her up here?"

I'm pretty sure she's covered her tracks. I mean, her dad didn't know about the scholarship. Unless. My gut freezes. "I never thought to ask if she'd left anything in her room about other applications. I know she applied to other universities too. If one of them sent her an acceptance letter – or any kind of letter – we're screwed."

"Maybe not," Anton says. "If one of the other universities wrote to her, and her dad checked them out, he'd find out she wasn't there. But that wouldn't give him a clue about where she might be."

"You think?" It's too much to hope for.

"There might be another option," Jeff says. Anton told me he was a chess player. It shows. He's thinking several moves ahead of everyone else, while we're running around like a bunch of mice fleeing from a herd of cats. "What would happen if she changed her name? Then if her dad did send out a query, or file a missing persons report, no one would link it to her."

It's a brilliant idea. Now all we need is for Sahira to call, so we can get it started.

We do all the ditzy stuff – figuring out what to have for dinner, who's going to cook etc. I'd happily have Jeff cook every meal – he's a great chef – but that's not fair to him. Unless I do something else in place of cooking. I look around his apartment. It looks like a guy's apartment – pretty barren, so there isn't much to create a mess. And it's basically clean, so there's not a lot I can contribute in that department. Still, there must be something.

Jeff notices me looking around. "Lost something?"

I blush. Jeez – when's the last time I did that? I try not to stutter when I tell him I'm just looking. He gives me that quizzical look – the one that says 'oh, really?' and then he laughs. "Okay. What's on your mind?"

"Just thought there might be something I could help you with. But everything looks pretty organized."

"Just on the surface. I've got about six library books that are going to be overdue if I don't get them back today. If you feel like going for a walk, I'd really appreciate getting them returned."

Well that's easy! He points to a stack of books, hands me a shopping bag and gives directions to the library. "Here," he says, handing me his card. "Use this if you see something you'd like to read while you're here."

While I'm here? Does he mean while I'm here for the weekend at his place, or while I'm here in Kamloops? If my original plan had worked out, I'd get my own library card. But there doesn't seem to be much point to it now.

I take his card anyway, scuff into my sneakers and head for the door. Before I reach it, the phone rings. Jeff grabs it.

"Hi, Jeff here…. Oh, hi Sahira. Glad you called. Hang on a minute."

He waves the phone at me and seconds later, Sahira's voice carves familiar patterns in my head. There's so much to say and I don't even know where to start.

Jeff wig-wags me. "Ask her to come for dinner – there's lots."

She turns down Jeff's invitation. "Thank him for me," she says. "But I've got another suggestion. Can you meet me at the Lunch Box? It's right across the street from the West Gate entrance. I can walk there from the residence, and it's an easy bus ride for you."

An hour later, we're exchanging hugs and talking a mile a minute trying to catch up. She's apologizing for screwing up my plan and I'm apologizing for not being a whole lot smarter about getting in touch with her.

While we eat, I try to figure out how to ask if she knows she's in danger. Every time I edge up to the question, she dances away from it. Finally I just blurt it out. "Sahira, do you think your dad knows where you are? Or how to find you?"

Her smile evaporates and her eyes grow cloudy. "No, I don't think so. I didn't leave a note or anything, and I haven't phoned or written to anybody. I think I'm okay here."

I'm relieved, but still concerned. "Anton wondered what might happen if you got an answer from one of the other universities. Would your dad open your mail?"

She laughs. "In a second. He opens all my mail anyway. Not that I ever got that much, but I can't remember anything that hadn't been opened before I got it. Not even a birthday card."

"But you got that acceptance letter. . ."

"You didn't read the envelope. I used the next door neighbor's address. I told them it was a surprise for my mom and they thought that was sweet. So they kept the letter for me and didn't tell her about it."

So her tracks are covered. I hope. It scares me that there's something I've overlooked that's going to screw up everything and put us back to square one.

"Look – this is hard, but I have to ask. What would happen if your dad found out where you were?"

There's a long pause before she answers. "I don't know. I'd like to think he wouldn't do anything, but I'm not sure that would be true. He's got an awful temper – you've never seen it, but sometimes…."

She stops. Whatever it is, she isn't going to tell me. I think I can guess, but I hope I'm wrong. The silence grows thicker. Now I'm really scared.

"You're all registered for the fall semester?" I fall back on small talk. Somehow I have to fill the void between us and maybe we can talk about the really important stuff later. When she feels a little more comfortable.

"Oh – yeah. I was too late to register for the summer session, but it was fun to sit in on courses and get a feel for the place. And I got a head start on some of the courses I'll be taking."

"Sounds like a good way to meet people."

She starts picking at her thumb nail. It's what she does when she doesn't really want to answer a question, or talk about something.

"Sahira, what's wrong?"

She shrugs. "I don't know – I just don't seem to be able to meet people easily. I can sit at the back of the room and watch everybody, but it's hard for me to walk up to someone and start talking to them." She looks around the restaurant. "Everybody else goes around smiling and talking to people, but I can't."

Maybe this is the time to get her thinking about creating a new persona. "Jeff had a good suggestion. How would you feel about changing your name?"

She looks at me, blankly.

"I mean, that way, even if your dad could trace you to Kamloops, or file a Missing Persons report, if your name was different, no one would know it was you."

The beginning of a smile curls her lips – then it disappears. "But how can I do that? Don't you have to have official documents of some sort?"

"Jeff seemed to think it wouldn't be that hard. Anyway, it's something to think about."

She surprises me.

"I don't have to think about it." She laughs. "I can be just like a Hollywood star! Now what kind of name should I pick? Am I going to sound glamorous? Or intelligent? Or what?"

Well, that was easier than I thought it would be.

She glances at her watch. "I should go – it'll get dark out pretty soon, and I don't like walking around by myself."

"Me neither."

We hug. It's an awkward hug – like the kind you give your great-aunt that you only see twice a year at family gatherings.

She breaks away. "How much longer will you be planting trees?"

"The last rotation starts in mid-September."

"The fall semester starts about then – a little while after Labour Day."

"Well, tree planters don't get holidays, so I'll be working on Labour Day, then have my days off and start my last rotation."

"What will you do when you're finished? Stay in Kamloops or head back home?"

"I don't know."

This is the hard part. I really don't know what I'm going to do. I know what I want to do – but it doesn't look like that's going to happen. It's clear that our original plan of living together isn't going to work out. She's happy living in residence and it makes life simpler for her. No worries about transportation or anything of that sort. But that leaves me on my own, and I'm not sure if I'm ready to do that yet.

She bends forward to give me a quick hug, then turns, picks up her bag and slings it over her shoulder.

"Gotta go. Great seeing you again."

"You too," I reply. The automatic words that tumble out of my mouth. There's so much we have to say to each other. So much to think about, so much we've shared – and so much we haven't shared. I hate to think it's all going to end here. I had such great plans – thought I'd solved all the problems – but nothing's turned out the way I wanted it to.

I guess things haven't turned out the way she wanted them to, either.

I watch her leave before I head out the door to the bus stop. For once, I'm in luck and I don't have to hang around waiting for the bus. It arrives seconds after I reach the bus stop. It feels like I'm on a roll – not only didn't I have to wait for the bus, there's even an empty seat! Once I'm settled, I realize I've still got Dad's letter in my pocket, so I open it.

Christie:

Just a quick note – Karli and I will come to Kamloops for your next days off. I've got Jeff's address, so we'll get a hotel room, then come over to see you. We should be there by about 9 o'clock.

Hugs
Dad

It's after nine already. Shit! I should have opened his letter before I galloped out the door. All I can hope is Jeff and Anton are there. I'm mentally willing the bus to go faster, but it lurches along, making every possible bus stop and traffic light. It's almost 9:30 by the time it reaches my stop and I can bail out and run the last couple of blocks to Jeff's place.

Dad's car is sitting at the curb, empty.

I can hear Karli giggle as I reach the door. Then Jeff and Anton join in. Sounds like they're playing some sort of game. The door swings open silently. They don't notice me come in. It's a wonderful scene. Everyone looks happy and relaxed, and Karli is at her bubbly best. She's the one who spots me.

"Christie!" Her arms fly up as she scrambles to her feet, ready for a hug.

She feels so good in my arms. I love this little girl as though she really way my sister.

Then it's Dad's turn. "Hi," he says, grabbing me and Karli in a bear hug. "Good to see you again."

He doesn't know *how* good it is to see him. I've missed him like crazy. He's been the one constant in my life – the one I can always depend on. The one who's always in my corner.

I look around. "Where's Tiff?"

"We'll talk about that later," he says. Then he points to Anton. "Karli insists she knows him, and that his name is William. What's that all about?"

Anton and I start to laugh. "I was in the park one day, and we met Anton there. You know how Tiff's always putting down people from other cultures. Or anybody who was 'different'. She doesn't know Anton isn't 'white', just that he's a friend of mine so I thought it would be easier if Karli couldn't give away anything about Anton. So – I told Karli that his name was William." I wave my hands, making little circles in the air. "Pure self-defense I guess, and probably pretty silly."

Dad gives a quirky sort of smile. "Yeah – Tiff's thinking was a little scrambled at times."

I start to say something, but he puts his finger on my lips. "Not now."

Karli stops giggling long enough to yawn – one of those deep, totally infectious yawns that reminds everyone in the room how late it is.

"I guess we better get back to the hotel," Dad says. "How'd it be if I took you all out to breakfast tomorrow morning?"

Who's going to turn down an offer like that? We agree to meet at the MacDonald's, on Notre Dame Drive. I smile – it seems as though every other street here is named after a university.

"Walk me to my car?" he asks. He tucks Karli into her car seat with her favourite teddy bear, strolls behind the car and stops, facing me. That's when he tells me that Tiff walked out on him.

"You mean she's left you?"

He nods.

"I didn't see it coming. She'd been a little grumpy lately, but she's been that way ever since she had Karli. It's just gotten worse and worse, and over the summer, it seemed she was unhappy about almost everything. And obviously, I was number one on the list.

"Funny, because at first she was so sweet and so caring. After all the strikeouts, all those girlfriends that drifted in and out, I thought I'd finally hit a homer when I found Tiffany. Then Karli came along and I thought it would be just like it was when you were born. I should have known better. You can't repeat a highlight, and your mom was definitely one of the most wonderful things that ever happened to me."

I put my arm around him. "I'm sorry, Dad."

"It's okay, kiddo. I can live with it. But there's not why I'm here. Tiff talked to Sahira's dad. When he asked about you, she told him you were in Kamloops. I went through the roof when I heard that, told her she had no business giving him that information. Her exact words were *'Well I didn't tell him where Sahira was, even though he's entitled to know.'* I can't believe how stupid she is. Either that or plain malicious."

He stops and looks out in the distance, like he's trying to decide what to say next.

"That was the start of a king-sized argument. At the end of it, she announced that she was tired of sitting around just waiting to get old. She wanted out, and she wanted out *right now*. I told her she was welcome to leave. I guess she expected me to beg her to stay, but by that time I was pretty fed up with her attitudes. There was something else, too. It wasn't until you left that I realized how much you looked after Karli. That was one of Tiff's complaints: she had to do everything – look after the house, do the shopping, get the meals, look after Karli, etc.etc. I told her that's what most women did, and that's when everything went sideways. She left the next morning. No note, no nothing."

"You mean she just abandoned Karli?"

"Not exactly abandoned – she left her with me."

"But Karli's not . . ."

As I bite off my words, he gives me a funny look.

"It's okay, Christie. I know Karli isn't mine."

"You know?"

"I've known right from the start." He stops, and I can almost hear his mind working. "Okay. This isn't something that most dads talk about with their daughters, but – your mom had a real bad time with you. Not when you were born, but before, while she was pregnant. There were several problems….well, we don't need to go into that now. Anyway, after you were born, we decided it was too dangerous for her to go through that again - once was enough. So, I had the little operation. Later, when your mom got sick, I was glad I'd done it, because another pregnancy would have created real problems – delayed treatment and that sort of thing. And besides – we had you. What more could we ask for? You were the best baby possible."

He grinned. My dad has a funny, lopsided grin. It makes him look like a little kid. He reached out and took my hand, squeezed it, then picked up the story. "When Karli told me she was expecting, I knew I wasn't the father, but it didn't matter. She seemed everything I wanted – gentle, caring – all that good stuff. But once she moved in, that person evaporated. At first I put it down to the pregnancy, but nothing improved after Karli arrived. It's my fault – I should have said something, or done something, but I didn't. Karli was a cute little kid, so I just pretended she was mine."

Then he looks at me. "But how did you know?"

It's my turn to be embarrassed. "Okay. You got me." I take a deep breath. "I snooped. One night when you and Tiff went out, she left the bedroom door open, and a dresser drawer partly open. I was going to close it, when I noticed a journal." I glance up, waiting for a thundercloud to burst. "I know – I shouldn't have looked. But I did. So that's how I found out."

He surprises me. He doesn't say anything about snooping, or private property or anything. Just mulls it over for a moment, then quietly makes a comment. "And you never thought to tell me?"

"Didn't seem to be much point. You liked Karli – heck, everyone likes Karli. So why rock the boat?"

He nods. "You were always good to her."

"Probably because I remember what it's like to be that age, and have no mother. Even when Tiff was there, she wasn't what you'd call a great mother. So, yeah, I sort of took her under my wing."

Dad's arms wrap around me. It's a wonderful, warm feeling, like he's blocking out the world and protecting me from everything. I could stay there, cuddled close to him, forever.

His chest rumbles against my ear. "I'd better get Karli into bed or she'll be cranky tomorrow."

I step back, pretending there aren't any tears in my eyes. "Okay. See you at breakfast."

He leans forward, plants a kiss on my forehead, then gets into the car. I watch his tail-lights until they disappear. I'm remembering all the times I had to look after Karli during the day, when Tiff came home empty handed from the 'shopping' trips. Where had she really been? It's not something I need to share with dad, but now I wonder if she's gone back to the guy who got her pregnant, or if someone else is involved.

Breakfast is one of those sad but sweet times. I know things have changed, but I'm not sure what's going to happen next. One thing I do know, is just how much I've come to love Karli. And I'll do anything to help protect her. Dad and Karli head back to town after breakfast while I finish my chores and get ready to return to camp the next morning.

CHAPTER FIFTEEN

THERE'S A WEIRD nostalgia that comes with planting your last tray of trees. A sense of '*I'll never do this again*' as you dig those last slits, and tamp those last seedlings into place. You tell yourself '*I'll never be in this place again*'. For this city gal, it's been an adventure, and my memory bank is overflowing. One of the things I'm really going to miss is the clean air. Not just clean, but pine scented. A huge change from the car-exhaust that permeates city air. And it's quiet. No traffic hum. None of the throbbing engines that give life to the city. It was hard to get used to that at first – I'd wake up in the middle of the night and wonder what was wrong, why couldn't I hear anything? I know won't take long before I start to miss that peaceful stillness when we get back town, but for now, I'm just enjoying it. Every bit of it.

It's been a tough summer in a lot of ways, but I stuck it out and I'm proud of myself for that.

Now it's time for everyone to pack up and go back to their regular routines. It seems like I'm the only one who doesn't have one. Sahira's settled in at the university, Anton's registered at UBC, but I'm nowhere. I can't stay with Jeff on a permanent basis, and anyway, there's no real reason to stay in Kamloops. With Tiff gone, going home is sounding pretty sweet. I didn't always think that way. For years, there was a steady stream of girlfriends at Dad's house and I didn't much like any of them. Then Tiff came, but now she's gone. I don't think Dad's looking for another girlfriend, so things will be more settled. At least, I hope that's what's going to happen. I'd hate for Karli to go through what I did, and that's what makes me decide that going home is going to be my best option.

When I tell Jeff I'm leaving, he's really nice about it. "Anytime you want to come back, you're welcome."

He doesn't say that he's glad to get his privacy back, or happy that we aren't cluttering up his apartment any more, but I'm sure it's true. He's a kind and gentle guy and he's been a good friend. I'll miss him. I know he's sorry that Anton is leaving, but neither of us mentions it. Anton, of course, is flying back. I'm sure his parents are happy to have him back in school. Well. Lucky for Anton, but that's not the way my life is going. I just have to accept things the way they are and hope I can make a go of my writing.

I phone Sahira to tell her when I'm going back to Vancouver, and we make a date for lunch on my last day, at the same coffee shop where we met before. When I get there, she's waiting, and bubbling with excitement. It's almost like she's a different person.

"Hey, girlfriend," she says. "I'm really going to miss you."

"I'll miss you too, Sahira."

She laughs. "You won't be able to call me that much longer."

"Wazzup?"

"I took Jeff's advice and changed my name. It's been kind of weird figuring out who I wanted to be, but now I've got it sorted out."

She pauses – okay, she's entitled to a bit of drama. I rap my fingers on the table top.

"Drumroll!"

"How do you like Cassandra Thompson?"

"Cassandra?"

"Everyone can call me Sandy – which is close enough to my own name that maybe I'll recognize it when someone talks to me. But I'll use Cassandra as my 'official' name, and that's different enough that it might fool anyone who's trolling for someone called Sahira or Sandy."

"Makes sense. And Thompson?"

"After the river. It's something strong and steady – and that sounded good to me. I got the forms to make it official but I need my parents to sign it if I'm under 19. There's no way that's going to happen, but my birthday's not that far away, and then I can do what I want. I need to get my birth certificate first, and I've already written away for it. Anyway, my birthday present to myself is going to be the official name change."

"So if I write to you, who do I address my letter to?"

"Cassandra Thompson. I told the registrar I'm changing my name, and from now on, I'll use Sandy Thompson."

"Can you do that, even before you change it?"

"Yeah – I checked it out." She puts her fingers in the air to make quotation marks. "The registrar said, 'As long as there's no fraudulent intent' – and this isn't fraud." She laughs. "I'll probably have to come up with a reason for changing my name. I can't put down the real reason, so I'll just say it's for personal reasons, and I need a copy of the name change to apply for a new passport. I'll need that for identification – I don't have a driver's license, so a passport is the next best form of identification, even if I'm not going anywhere." She pauses for a moment, and shakes her head. "I can't believe how many times I have to show some identification. Some of it for the silliest things. Anyway, the passport will solve that problem.

"When I first read through the form, where it asked why I was changing my name, I was going to say it was because of numerology. I think there's a lot to it, but I don't think a government office would accept that as a valid reason." She looks at me for a moment. "You know, when you study it – and I did get really interested in it for a while, there are a lot of people – famous people – who've changed their names, and it's made a huge difference in their lives."

"Wow! If numerology works, maybe I should change my name too. Think it would help if I changed it to J.K.Rowling or Judy Blume?"

Sahira takes my hand. "Hey, girlfriend – they had their day. Believe in yourself, and keep at it, and you'll have yours."

I'm touched. She's never said anything like that before. Lunch ends on a good note. I feel better about leaving her here.

On the bus, headed to Vancouver, I think about how our lives have changed in just a few short months. Sahira's so smart, she'll do really well at TRU. And I know she'll make new friends. It'll just take a little time. I laugh when I think about her new name. Sandy – that's pretty clever. And Thompson, for the university. I hope she does get a part time job somewhere on campus – not just for the money, but as a way to meet people. And give her a little more self-confidence. She's still got a lot to learn about being independent, but having her own money – even if it's not much – is going to help her. Some things haven't changed. Anton's still following the career path his parents chose for him, and he hasn't been able to convince them he's gay. Or maybe he's just comfortable going along for the ride, and he'll come out at some future date. I have no idea how that's going to happen, or what his parents might do, but they're so happy to have him home again that they even bought him that new car. How lucky can you get?

Dad's made it clear that I'm welcome to come home and I spend a little time thinking about where I might be able to set up a den or have a quiet corner somewhere, with a desk and maybe a bookshelf, to keep my writing stuff all in one place. Not like when I used to do my homework on the kitchen table after dinner, and bundle it all up to take back to school the next day. Dad isn't going to charge me rent or anything, so I've got my summer wages to play with. I didn't make as much as I'd hoped, but I am a couple of thousand dollars ahead. That will pay for a new computer and a desk – once I find a place to put it.

The trip goes quickly. Before I know it, I see the big IKEA sign, as the bus pulls in to the Port Coquitlam Depot – and Dad and Karli are waiting for me.

It's strange to sleep in my own bed again after spending the summer alternating between an air mattress in a tent, and the bunk bed at Jeff's place. My bed is nice. Comfortable and all that – but the night is noisy. Cars and trucks stream down the highway. Sirens cut through the traffic. Trains whistle as they haul their hundred plus trail of cars along the tracks. There are other noises – things I never noticed before, but after the quiet nights in the bush, they grab my attention. It's light out, as well. In camp, when the generator was turned off, it was dark. Nothing but the stars and moon – although sometimes the moonlight was strong enough to light up the landscape and cast long shadows. Here, it's always light. Street lights, neon lights, lights from the highway – it's never completely dark. And there are only half as many stars. I know the answer to that: the ambient light means stars have to be brighter before you can see them, so the less bright stars I could see in the bush, are invisible here. I'm not sure it's a good trade.

It's been a very long night and I didn't get much sleep, so I'm happy when the dark recedes and there's daylight again. I revel in my shower - a long, long shower - and shampoo my hair twice to get rid of the smell of pine needles and campfire smoke and sweat. It's a treat to open my dresser drawers and have piles of clean clothing to wear. But now I have to make choices. In camp, it was easy – jeans and a sweat shirt or shorts and a tee shirt. Now I've got stacks of jeans, shorts, chinos, cords – it's almost overwhelming. Plus a couple of drawers full of tee shirts, tank tops, camisoles and other stuff to wear on top.

Funny – all the time I was out in the bush, I missed the things I had at home, and now that I'm home, I miss the things I had in the bush. The peace, the quiet and the simplicity.

I shake my head. Okay, Christie. Let's get the show on the road. Enough lollygagging – time to go downstairs, see Dad and Karli and figure out what you're going to do with your life. Great. Now I'm talking to myself. That's definitely a bad sign!

Dad has breakfast all ready. The waffle iron is heated and ready, bacon's sizzling in the pan, coffee is perking – and there's even pink grapefruit, cut and ready to enjoy.

"Looks good, Dad," I say, giving him a quick hug.

"Gotta say welcome home to my girl," he smiles.

"I set the table," Karli announces.

"Good for you," I say, picking her up and twirling her around. "I guess we make a pretty good family, don't we?"

Later, Dad and I talk about where I can set up a study. "If I re-arrange my room, there's enough space for a desk," I say. But he's got other ideas. He wants to build something in the back yard.

"Like a playhouse?"

He laughs. "I guess you could call it that – but I had in mind something a little bigger than a playhouse."

"Can I have one too?" Karli asks.

"No reason why both of my girls can't have something special."

He's already drawn up plans and he rolls them out on the table to show me. It's like he knew all along I'd be coming home again. This isn't a playhouse, it's a miniature house that you could almost live in. Basically it's one main room, with a washroom and a mini-kitchen. "I thought we could put in a half-size fridge – like the ones in hotel rooms – and a hot plate or something," he says.

Not that I'm feeling any pressure or anything, but at this moment, I can almost see what's in my dad's mind: him beaming as I produce best-seller after best-seller, right there in our own back yard. It's a little overwhelming, to say the least.

"Dad – that's a wonderful idea, but for now, can I just put a desk in my bedroom? Or maybe can I set up a study in the rec room? That would be a super space. Anyway, you won't be able to build anything until springtime, and I need to get set up sooner than that."

"You can build my house now," Karli chirps.

"No, Christie's right. This isn't a good time of year to build houses – big ones or little ones," Dad says. "We'll have to wait until springtime to build anything, and anyway, it's too cold in the winter for you to use a playhouse. When springtime comes, I'll build your house first, and then make Christie's 'office'."

I know the kind of house he's thinking of getting for Karli. Costco has them, all ready to assemble. Last year, he and Tiff argued about getting one. Dad wanted to, she didn't. It seemed weird at the time, 'cause you'd think it would be the other way around. But looking back, Tiff didn't like dad spending money on anyone other than her. Not even her own daughter.

"Hey, Karli – how about you share the rec room with me? You can have one corner and I'll have another."

She beams. Too bad more problems can't be solved that easily.

After breakfast, I turn on my computer. It's one of dad's old ones – old and slow. I wait what seems like forever for it to warm up, bleep, blip and finally produce images on the screen.

There's a message from Sahira "Welcome home, girlfriend."

It's great to be back in touch with her, and I laugh as I send back a reply. "Hey – there's something to be said for a bed with clean sheets."

Now comes the part I've been looking forward to all summer. I write out a cheque, for the same amount as Dad gave me, put it in an envelope and address it to him. I put it on the mantelpiece – standing up against the mirror, so he'll notice it. Then I wait. And wait. Jeez – won't he *ever* find it? Eventually he does.

"What's this?"

"That's what I owe you. I told you I'd pay you back."

"You don't have to, Christie. That was a gift."

"Nope. It was a loan. That's what we agreed."

"You're almost as stubborn as I am, aren't you?" But he's laughing as he says it.

"Sometimes."

"Okay. Tell you what. You wanted a new computer – why don't we go get one. We can use this."

I look at him. "Now who's being stubborn?"

"You got me. But seriously – I know the one you've got needs to be updated. It was slow when I gave it to you and I'm sure it hasn't speeded up any since then."

We head out to the computer stores – and there are lots of them. It seems like every mall has a couple of stores. Walmart and Best Buy and Costco and lots of others. We start looking at all the new models and I'm blown away by how many different kinds there are. Everything from featherweight tablets and I-pads to desk top models.

"Maybe we should have done some homework first," Dad groans.

"Probably – but it's more fun to look at the real article. Plus, I can try out the keyboards and see how they feel. Can't do that when you're searching online."

"Can I get one too?" Karli asks. They have some really great computers for little kids – colourful, sturdy – and programs to help them learn.

Dad and I look at each other, and he smiles. "I think we can afford two."

* * *

Sahira's doing okay too. Whoops! Sandy's doing okay. Her e-mail last week was a real high.

> *I've got a job! Yes! Working in the library. I'm in the stacks. That's library talk for the book shelves. Regular librarians handle all the returns, then the librarians pile them on big carts. That's when*

grunts, like me, get to wheel the carts along and put the books back on the shelves in the right places. Just think, 12 years of education and what really pays off is something I learned in Grade One – the alphabet!

She talks about joining the badminton club too. More power to her.

Karli's been a real sweetie. Dad has her in kindergarten for the morning, and she goes to daycare in the afternoon.

"We could save a bunch of money if I looked after Karli instead of using daycare," I suggest as Dad and I put dinner together.

We'd been laughing and joking, but he suddenly turns serious.

"That wouldn't be fair to you, and it wouldn't be fair to Karli."

"I wouldn't mind . . ."

He cuts me off. "No. You're not going to be a surrogate mother. Not just because you have other things to do, but I'm really thinking of Karli right now. She's had too many changes already. You went to Kamloops. Her mom left. Those were two pretty big events for a little girl. I put her in kindergarten, and daycare. She's got the beginnings of a routine established, and I think it's important that we don't throw any more changes at her. She loves being with you, and that's great, but you need your freedom and Karli needs some structure."

"Is that why you put her in kindergarten?"

"Partly. It wasn't until after you left, that I realized how little Tiffany did with her. Karli's days mostly involved watching television. Not Sesame Street or educational programs but junk shows. Daytime talk shows and soap operas. When I finally paid attention to what Karli could do – no, that's not right. It was when I realized what she *couldn't* do – that I realized something was very wrong. And when I compared that with what you could do at that age, I could see there was a huge gap."

I'm really glad dad took over. Karli's a neat little kid, and she wasn't getting much from Tiff.

"There's something else we need to talk about," he continues. "And that's about those damned stickers on my car. I'm glad you got past the red L, because everybody thought *I* was the learner, but I'm really getting fed up with the green N. I'm not a new driver, and I hate it when people look at me funny and swing wide to pass.

"I want you to take that sticker off my car. Enough's enough." He glares for a minute, then starts to laugh. "So put it on your own car."

It takes a minute to sink in. "My own car?"

He grins. "Yep."

I give him the biggest bear hug ever. "Really? You're not kidding me?"

"Nope. We'll look around and see what we can find. It won't be a brand new one, but you're going to need some reliable transportation."

He's right. I've signed up for a writing course at the college, and I've joined a fitness club. So a car would be really great to get around. I don't mind using my bike on nice days, but it's too dangerous in the rain – and we get a lot of rainy days in the winter. Besides, with a car, I can help out with the shopping, and picking up Karli from daycare. I can hardly wait to tell Sahira. Shit. How long is it going to take before I stop saying that and start thinking of her as Sandy?

Her email response is lukewarm, to say the least.

"That's nice." Then she goes on to talk about stuff she's doing.

That's her whole comment on my car! Fuck. If things were the other way around, I'd be bouncing off the ceiling. I'd be so happy for her I wouldn't be able to control myself. I'd have a million questions. Well, okay, I might not know too much about cars, but at least I'd want to know what year it is, and what colour. But Sandy doesn't ask a single question. Two words. That it, and then she goes on to talk about her stupid badminton club and the nifty racquet she got at the on-campus garage sale. Whoop-dee-do. I guess I shouldn't be surprised – she was never really keen on driving. When we were in Grade Ten, the school had a Driver Ed course. I tried to talk her into taking it with me, but her dad wouldn't sign the permission slip. That finished it. Her mom doesn't drive, so she never had much of a role model that way. There are a lot of things that her mom doesn't do – I hope Sandy gets past that. She'll have to, now that she's on her own.

We settle into our new routine. Karli loves kindergarten and brings home a freshet of pictures she's coloured, words she's traced and the numbers she's learned. Dad puts them all on the fridge at first, but they quickly overflow, so after a hilarious 'consultation' they decide to pick the best one each week, and mount it in a special frame Dad made, with little magnets on the back to hold it in place.

After a pretty chaotic summer, Dad's back at work. He works with a developer – he doesn't sell houses or anything like that. It's something to do with finding places to put new complexes and shopping centres and that sort of thing. Or maybe it's finding places and deciding what should go into them. Sometimes he works from home, but he does have a real office in the mall, and he can spend a lot of time there when he gets really busy. I asked him once, what he actually did. His response was pure Dad.

"I get paid for day-dreaming."

I'm not quite sure how that works, but he seems to like what he does and it pays pretty good. At least, it seems to. I know there's no mortgage on our house, and any time we need something, there's no hassle.

While Dad and Karli are getting on with their lives, I'm back at school. No one was more surprised than me when I registered at the college, but after trying to write and getting nowhere, I decided that a little formal instruction wouldn't hurt. The course is interesting – we get assignments every week, and I'm learning a lot about writing. Enough to know that I'm nowhere near ready to start a book yet. Aside from not having a serious idea about a story line, there are all the technical things involved. Things like building scaffolding for a story, then making sure no one can see it. That puzzled me when I first heard it, but then I realized it was like constructing a frame for a building, and then covering it up. It gives strength and support but isn't obvious. Good stories need that too, and I'm beginning to recognize some of the things we talk about in class in some of the books we're assigned to read. And we've graduated from paragraphs and vignettes to short stories. Dad keeps asking to see them, but I'm not ready for that yet.

"Okay, kiddo – let me know when you are, and I'll make another frame for the fridge."

I really miss Sandy, but we keep in touch. She's playing lots of badminton, and gobbling up her course work. That doesn't surprise me. The girl is brilliant. She's still working in the library and they've given her a few more hours, so she's started a bank account.

"What's it for?" I ask.

She e-mails back. *This is for when I go to Saskatchewan. After I leave here, I'll have to do some veterinarian courses and the university there has pretty great qualifications. I have to pay for that myself – no more scholarships, at least not yet – but that's okay. Maybe I can get lucky and qualify for some kind of assistance. But for now, the main thing is to finish here and get really good marks."*

Talk about focus! I'd be thinking about new clothes, or maybe a trip somewhere. Or even a personal computer. But not Sandy. She's still working on the library computers and happy to slop around in sweats. Oh – and buy fresh birdies for badminton. At least she's happy, and she's safe.

Anton's something else altogether. He drops by the house quite often now, just to visit, to play with Karli and, I think, to hang with my Dad. He's getting good marks at school, but he hates every course he's taking.

"If I won the lottery, I'd walk out of every class and sign up for the theatre program. That's what I really want to do."

We both know there's no chance of that as long as his parents are paying his bills. Anyway, he never buys lottery tickets, so that's never going to happen.

Somehow, the time whizzes by. Hallowe'en comes and goes before I'm anywhere near ready for it. Karli goes trick-or-treating as a cat-person, wearing a cat-suit with a swishy tail, and little whiskers drawn on her face. Dad takes her out while I stay home, answering the doorbell and handing out treats.

Almost overnight, the leaves change colours – fantastically beautiful until a rainstorm hits and howling winds bring them down, turning them into soggy brown piles that have to be cleared away from the drains.

Next thing I know, it's almost Christmas.

"Still nothing for the fridge?" Dad asks. It's a running joke. Every week when he posts Karli's stuff, he asks about mine. It's coming, but I'm not sure if I'm ready to let him see it yet. It's different in class – I know the kinds of comments our instructor is going to make, and what others in the class are going to say. We've been well coached in what you do and don't say in a critique. Even a negative critique is okay, as long as it points out a flaw and doesn't just say 'this story sucks'. As we learned in the first week, you can learn almost as much from a poorly written story, as you can from a well-crafted one. More, sometimes, because with the really well-crafted ones, you don't see what went into making them so powerful and so interesting. The crappy ones have their bones sticking out.

The semester ends with a flurry of 'see you next spring' and 'let's get together over Christmas', except for a couple of kids who won't be coming back. That reminds me of Sahira, who won't be coming back at Christmas, and I really, really miss her. We used to have such fun at Christmas, making all sorts of stuff. For a few years, we were really into hand-made gifts and cards. I've still got some of the cards she did for me, and a pair of slippers she knitted. They don't fit, and they're not quite the same size, but I wouldn't part with them for anything.

I got a 'well done' on my last story, and I'm going to copy it out to put in Dad's stocking. Not a real present – I'll get something to put under the tree – but maybe he'll get a kick out of the story.

Karli's out of kindergarten and out of daycare for the holidays, so we get to spend lots of time together. Nobody builds houses or plans developments over Christmas, so Dad's home too and it's really great for the three of us, to just be a family.

I asked Dad once, if he ever heard from Tiff.

"Nope. And I can't say I'm sorry."

I don't know what their official status is, but for now, he seems happy just being Dad to Karli and me. There's a little voice in the back of my head that says, "*You can't trust Tiff. She could decide to come back, or she could ask for custody of Karli, and child support payments.*" Sometimes that worries me, and other times I think it's just my author voice butting in, making plot twists that aren't necessary in real life. I mean, they happen, but Dad used to say that worrying about something that hasn't happened yet is borrowing trouble. I guess he's right. But I still don't trust Tiff.

There's a humungous e-mail from Sahira. Whoops! Sandy. It isn't hard to look behind the words and see that she's lonesome, but she's keeping busy.

> "The badminton club has closed for the holidays, so I thought I'd go to a gym, just for fitness training. And guess what? They wanted someone part-time to help out over the holidays, to keep the little kids busy while their moms are in class. So – I do that for a couple of hours a day on Monday, Wednesday and Friday. In return, I get my membership for free. Pretty good deal!"

She talks about some of the foreign students at TRU, who can't go home for the holidays.

> "They've been 'adopted' by some of the instructors and I've been invited to come along on a couple of trips. We're going skiing, which is going to be pretty funny for some of them. Preeta is from Fiji and she was telling me that for Christmas, her family usually has a picnic on the beach. She'd never seen snow before she came here. She's seen pictures of it, but she's never made a snowman, had a snowball fight, or been on skiis. I've never been on skiis either, so that's going to be fun for both of us."

All too soon, the holidays are over. Dad loved the short story I gave him, so I guess I'm learning something after all. Karli is happy to go back to kindergarten and daycare, Sahira's back in class, and I'm into a new semester at the college. The only person who isn't happy is Anton, but that's his problem. He's joined the drama club at UBC and he's trying out for the spring production, but he's not very hopeful about getting chosen for one of the parts.

"It pretty much all goes to the kids who are doing theatre majors,' he says. "That's not me." He's still having problems at home, but his parents still keep paying the bills.

"One of these days, you're going to have to shit or get off the pot," I tell him.

"Yeah. I know. But it's a tough call."

Then he gets a funny look on his face, like he's dialed out and gone somewhere else.

"Earth to Anton, Earth to Anton. Come in please."

"Sorry. Know what I was thinking about? Last summer, in Kamloops. I think that was the most fun I've had in my whole life." Then he laughs. "Yep – in spite of all the complaining I did, it was really great. I loved being on my own, I even loved the hard work."

"Are you going back this summer?"

"I think I will. How about you?"

There's no easy answer to that. I'd love to see Sahira again – but remembering last year, when we spent most of our time in the bush – I know that if I did go, we wouldn't be able to spend much time together. Now that I've got a car, it would be easier to drive up and spend a few days together. Maybe on a long weekend or something. I'd hoped to go up sometime during the winter, but Dad put the kibosh on that

"The roads can be icy, and it can be really dangerous. And anyway, you don't have snow tires. Better wait till the weather's better."

I bring my mind back to Anton's question. A few months ago, I would have signed up in a second. But things have changed for me, and know that the answer I give him isn't the one he's looking for.

"Not sure. I might be staying here for the summer semester. I've got a couple of ideas I want to work on."

"Oh. Well, that should be interesting." He doesn't quite make a face, but almost. I'm sorry to disappoint him.

"Are you still in touch with Jeff?"

"Yep. He's talking about coming down over Easter."

"Staying with you?"

He nods. "Yeah. I'm hoping he can help me get through to my parents."

I don't ask the obvious question – what then? Would they keep paying Anton's bills once they have to acknowledge that he's gay? Or would they be so upset they'd kick him out of the house? In either case, it's bound to be a pretty dramatic event. Dramatic and traumatic for both parties. That might be an interesting theme for a story. I file it away in the back of my mind.

I change the subject. "I'm going to drive up for a weekend, once the roads are clear. Want to come?"

He looks at me – almost in awe. "Hey – you're really getting into this driving thing, aren't you?"

"Use it or lose it."

"I don't think that applies to cars."

"I know – I'm just being silly. But yeah, I really do like driving."

He shakes his head. "Lucky you. I've hardly used my car at all. It's just easier to take the bus out to UBC – no parking hassles- and it actually saves money. I think it even saves time, too, because the bus drops me where I want to go and I don't have to walk back and forth from the parking lot to the buildings." He looks at me for a minute. "Are you serious about driving up to Kamloops?"

"Sure. Interested?"

"Yeah. I think I am. I could help with the driving if you wanted."

I shrug. "Whatever. How about setting it up for spring break?"

This is going to be so cool! I can see Sandy, he can see Jeff, and I can play with my toy. Help with the driving? No way! He's not going to touch my steering wheel.

* * *

It's Spring Break! The weather is great, the roads are clear and dry, and the e-mails have been flying back and forth between me, Anton, Sahira and Jeff. They're full of plans – things to do, places to go. I can tell it's going to be a busy few days. I bounce out of bed, ready to hit the road.

"Hey there," Dad says. "You're not leaving without breakfast?"

"I'll get something once we're underway. Maybe stop at Hope."

"You can stop at Hope if you want to, but you're not leaving the house without something in your stomach. Come on, settle down."

He's right. Of course he's right. But I'm still impatient to get going.

"Coffee and toast. Can we compromise on that?"

Now Karli gets into the act. "Can I have raising toast?"

"Raisin," I say. "Not raising."

"Okay," she says. "And I want peanutbutter'n'honey on it."

That's her latest favourite – peanut butter mixed with honey. I tried it a couple of times and it's pretty good, but I still prefer peanut butter and banana.

We finally finish breakfast, clear the table and put stuff away. I head out to the driveway to load up the car. To be honest, it isn't much of a load. I've got one small bag, my running shoes, and one pair of dressy flats, in case we go out anywhere. Dad looks at me – I know he's got a couple of hundred things to warn me about – don't speed, don't follow too closely, don't forget to signal, check your gas, etc.etc.etc. That's not even starting on the things he'll want to warn me about in Kamloops. Instead, he just grins.

"Have a good trip. Phone me when you get to Kamloops."

Dad and Karli wave me off and I head over to Anton's place. He's waiting for me, his backpack on the sidewalk at his feet.

He flags me down, like he's calling a taxi. I laugh and pop the trunk for his bag.

"Where to, mister?"

"Kamloops," he says, with a grin, sliding into the passenger seat.

We're underway. It feels like we're playing hooky. Anton's got a mile-wide grin on his face, and I guess I have too. We laugh at everything along the way, read out all the silly signs we see, and the funny bumper stickers. I think the best one is "Really? Imagine that!" but Anton likes the one that says "My other car is a tank." We sing along with the radio, making up verses when we don't know the words.

"You should be a songwriter," I tell Anton. "You're good at this."

"I'd like to be a songwriter. I'd probably do better as a songwriter than a singer."

He didn't get a part in the spring play at UBC – too bad, because I think he would have been great. He was flying high after the auditions, but came down with a thump when they announced the casting and he wasn't on the list. Not even as an understudy.

I tried to console him. "Come on – that's not positive thinking. You *know* why you didn't get a part."

"Yeah – I know. I'm not in the arts program. And I probably wouldn't have been any good anyway." He grimaced, like he'd tasted something that had gone bad. "Anyway, just to be practical, I wouldn't have had the time for rehearsals even if I did get it. My course load is pretty heavy and it isn't going to get any lighter."

He's hanging on to an A- average, and hoping to pull it up to a full A. So I guess he really doesn't have much spare time anymore.

We stop for lunch at the A&W in Princeton. Anton gets a Papaburger, and sweet potato fries. I'm happy with a root beer float. I don't know what it is about A&W root beer, but it's been my favourite ever since I was a little kid. Especially with a couple of scoops of ice cream in it.

While he's munching away on his burger, I pop bubbles in my float, and sip it slowly. Then I reach over to steal one of his fries. I've never had the sweet potato fries before but now I wish that I'd ordered some too. They're really great.

I can't believe how much Anton eats without gaining weight. If I even *looked* at half of what he consumes, I'd be way over 80 kgs in no time flat.

"Want me to drive?" he asks, as we finish our lunch.

"Nope, I'm good, thanks."

He grins. He was the same way when he got his car.

"Okay. Take it away."

We get back on the highway and the kilometers click by pretty quickly. It's not like last year, when everything was new and strange. In a way, I almost feel like I'm coming home.

CHAPTER SIXTEEN

IT'S A PRETTY drive up through the parks, but it's really different than going up on the bus. I don't have time to look at anything because I'm paying attention to the road. Driving conditions are good – the road is bare and dry, but I still get goosebumps when some of those big trucks pass me. Maybe when I've been driving for a zillion years, I'll be a little more relaxed around them.

When we're just past Merritt, a little more than an hour from Kamloops, I start rolling my shoulders and reminding myself to sit up straighter.

Anton looks at me. "Sure you don't want me to spell you off?

I wanted to do the whole thing by myself, but there's no point in being stupid. Tight fingers of tension are cramping my back, and pulling at my shoulders. It's time for a break. I answer Anton, without taking my eyes off the road. "Yeah, I guess I do. We'll switch at the next pull-out."

Minutes later, the road widens. I flick on my turn signal, edge into the outer lane, then cruise to a stop. It isn't until I get out that I realize how tired I actually am. Anton climbs out and starts doing some of the yoga stretches we learned last summer.

"Don't laugh," he says. "They really work."

"I'm not laughing," I tell him, joining in. We probably look pretty goofy to drivers passing by, but right now, I don't care what we look like. It just feels good to stretch out and loosen up those tight muscles.

A few minutes later, we pull out. Just near the Logan Lake cutoff there's a couple of police cars, a strip beside the road marked off with yellow tape and a flag-person directing traffic into a single lane corridor around the scene.

"Somebody's day has gone sideways," Anton says. I can't see anything on the road, no broken glass or debris, but something's happened. We're only a few minutes out of Kamloops now, and Anton turns to me for directions.

"Did you google a map?"

"Yeah. We can go to Jeff's first to let you off, and I'll drive to the university by myself."

I feed him directions, and before long, we pull up in front of Jeff's apartment block. Jeff must have been watching out the window, because he waves when he spots the car and exits the building moments later.

It's good to see him again. We chat for a minute while Anton pulls his pack from the trunk.

"I know you want to get to the university," Jeff says, giving me a hug. "Say hi to Sahira for me. Are we good for breakfast tomorrow?"

I nod my head. I start to ask if I can bring anything, when Jeff continues.

"This is a special occasion – so let's all meet at the Lunch Box Café. They serve a great breakfast – and no one has to do dishes." By that time, Anton's got his pack out and rejoined us.

"Sounds good to me."

"Right", Jeff grins. "See you both at 8 o'clock." He pauses, then adds, "Sharp."

I give him a salute and say, "Aye, aye, sir," then climb back in the car.

Jeff and Anton walk into the building and I head over to my hotel. I reserved a double room at Days Inn, near the campus, so Sahira and I can spend a few days together. There's a mall nearby, with restaurants, all kinds of funny little stores and boutiques if we want to shop, and lots of other things to do and see in and around Kamloops. I didn't have much time to play tourist last summer, so this is going to be fun.

When I check in, I ask for my messages.

"Sorry, there aren't any."

"None?"

Wordlessly, he shakes his head and shrugs his shoulders.

"Okay. Thanks." I grab my key and haul my bag up to the room. It looks okay. Standard hotel room, but nice and clean. I look out at the traffic on the street. Pretty quiet. But then, I guess I'm used to traffic on the Lower Mainland, and it's always a zoo. I put my bag on the bed and head out. I'll pick Sahira up at the university, and then we can decide where we want to eat.

It only takes a few minutes to drive up to TRU, park at the residences and enter the building.

There's a clerk at the desk. She looks up, and smiles brightly. I'm guessing she's a student, working a few hours a week to get a little extra money.

"Can I help you?"

I smile back. "I'm meeting my girlfriend here. Can you ring her room and let her know I'm here? Or do I just go up?" I'm not sure what the protocol is, and I know some places have pretty strict security.

"What's her cell number?"

"She doesn't have one. Her name is Sandy Thompson."

The girl laughs. "I remember her. We were teasing her about her name – and how great it must be to have a river and a university named after you."

I wait patiently.

"I haven't seen her today. Does she know you're coming?"

"Yes."

"We don't have phones in the rooms, and I can't let you upstairs. I'm sorry – we're shorthanded today. There's usually two of us here, but my partner isn't here today."

We're at an impasse, each waiting for the other to do something, but nothing happens. Finally, she turns back to her computer. "When one of the other students goes up, I'll ask her to knock on Sandy's door."

With no other option, I walk over to the waiting area and slump into a chair. Maybe she's still at the library, doing homework or whatever. I think about looking for her, but realize that if we're both wandering around the campus looking for each other, it's a good way to miss one another completely.

I check my watch again. It's almost 7:30 – she'll probably be back soon. I pick up a tattered magazine and glance through it. It's about six months out of date and all about fashion. Bo-ring. I take out my cell and text a message to my dad. It's now 7:40.

I go back to the desk. "Isn't there any way of checking her room? Or could I just go up?" I ask.

"Sorry, but I can't leave the desk and we're not allowed to let unauthorized persons upstairs."

If she says 'sorry, but…' one more time, I might scream.

Luckily she can't read my mind, and carries on. "I'm sure someone will be going -- oh, here's Karen. She's just a couple of doors down from Sandy's room."

Karen listens for a minute, then smiles. "Sure. I'll check for you." She's back much too quickly. "Sorry. No answer. She must have gone out."

"Thanks."

I watch the hands on the clock crawl around to 8 o'clock, then 8:30. I'm starting to get ticked off. She knew I was coming, and I told her I'd be here around 7 o'clock to pick her up so we can take her stuff to the motel and then go for dinner. So where is she?

The clerk leaves her desk and walks toward me. "Sorry, but I'll have to ask you to leave now. We close the doors at 9 o'clock."

"But…" There's nothing to say. Sahira doesn't have a cell, she isn't in her room, and I have no way of knowing where she might be, or when she might return.

"Can I leave a message for her?"

"Sure."

I pull the hotel receipt from my bag and check the phone number and room number, write them on a slip of paper, then sign it. "Give this to her, please."

"I'll put it on the notice board," she says, scooping a thumb tack out of a container on the desk. "There. Everyone checks the board when they come in."

That's progress. It's the first time she's said something without prefacing it with 'sorry, but…'.

Pulling my car out of the parking lot, I head back to the hotel, fuming. What now? Just sit in the hotel and wait for her to call? Once in the room, I turn on the TV, but there's nothing on except a string of stupid commercials. Maybe it's just the station break or something, but I'm too annoyed to sit and wait for the programs. I snap the TV off, and phone Jeff to see if Sahira's called him. She hasn't.

I'm really baffled by her behaviour. I'm getting mad, I'm getting worried, but I'm also getting tired. It was a long drive. Maybe I'll just lie down for a few minutes, and wait for her to call.

* * *

Sunlight pours through the window, waking me from a sound sleep. When was the last time I fell asleep in all my clothes? It doesn't feel good. I head for the shower, scrub, do my hair and come out wrapped in one of those super-sized hotel towels. Someday, I'm going to buy towels like that, when I have my own place. I sift through my bag, figuring out what to wear, before I realize it'll make more sense to check and see what Sahira wants to do. I pick up the phone and ask the desk to check for my messages. I can't imagine why Sahira didn't show up yesterday, but it's bound to be a good story – something we can laugh at.

"Sorry, there are no messages," the voice tells me.

"But there has to be?"

"Sorry. Nothing here."

I'm really getting worried now. I head back to the student residence, and check again. She's still not there, and my note is still pinned to the board. Something's going on. Several students are standing in the common room, huddled together. I wonder what's happened, but I don't have time to waste. It's 8 o'clock, and I should be at the restaurant meeting Jeff and Anton for breakfast. Correction. *We* should be at the restaurant. I drive over and dash into the café. There they are – sitting in a booth, enjoying a coffee while they study the menu. They smile as I walk in.

"Where's Sahira?" Anton asks.

"That's my question. She wasn't at the university last night and she didn't answer the message I left. I don't know where she is."

We look at each other, waiting for someone to make a suggestion – but no one can think of anything. I don't know her friends here – don't know where she might be – or why she's stood me up.

"You don't suppose something's happened, do you?" Jeff's face is concerned, but as usual, he's trying to find a logical answer to a problem.

"I don't know. I guess it's possible. But how would we find out?"

"If she's sick, or if there's been an accident, we could check the hospital and see if she's there," Anton says.

Breakfast is forgotten. Jeff throws some money on the table and we walk out. "We'll take my car," he says. "I know the way and it's easier if we all go together. We can come back for your car later."

It's only a five minute drive, but it seems to take forever. We park and look for the reception desk.

"Excuse me," Jeff says, catching the eye of one of the women standing at the back of the area.

"Can you help us? One of our friends has gone missing, and we just thought she might have gotten sick."

"I can check for you. What's your friend's name?"

"Sandy. Sandy Thompson. Or she might be under Cassandra."

She clicks across her computer screen, then looks up. "Sorry, no one has been admitted by that name." Then she smiles. "Well, that's probably good news, isn't it?"

We thank her, and leave, standing outside in the sunshine, trying to figure out what comes next. Do we go to the police? What do we tell them? How long does it take before someone is officially 'missing'? While we're debating, a delivery van pulls up and the driver hops out, dragging a bundle of newspapers. He loads them into the vending box, places one behind the glass, to show the front page, then leaves, whistling, to deliver the rest of his load.

Our eyes swing to the stark black letters headlining the front page.

"TRU STUDENT DIES IN MVA"

My stomach sinks. The floor lurches and I grab onto Anton.

"Please," I whisper. "Please. Don't let it be her."

Jeff finally moves, takes some coins from his pocket and plugs them into the machine. He opens the door and slips a paper out, flipping it over to read under the fold. "Oh, Jeez. It is. It's Sandy."

I grab the paper from him and start to read, my brain unwilling to accept what my eyes are telling me.

> *"Sahira Kaur Grewal, 19, was pronounced dead on arrival at Royal Inland Hospital early this morning, following a single vehicle accident late last night. Police say the car Ms. Grewal was driving left the road and plunged into the river.*
>
> *"Our investigation is not yet complete," a police spokesman said. "It's possible she veered to avoid hitting an animal. She was not wearing a seat belt. Preliminary investigation indicates Grewal was driving with a learner's license but was alone in the vehicle."*
>
> *An autopsy is scheduled for later today.*

"That doesn't make sense. It's crazy. Sahira didn't drive. Didn't want to drive. Has never driven. How could…" I run out of words as the room starts to spin.

Anton grabs me, folding me in his arms. "Hey, girlfriend. Hang on." I let myself feel the strength from his arms, and take a couple of deep breaths.

"Thanks. I'm okay now."

He quirks his eyebrow up, and twists his mouth into a grin, but he doesn't let go of me. His voice rumbles in his chest. "Hey, I'm upset too. This is pretty scary. I know she didn't drive before, but maybe she wanted to surprise you and didn't tell you she was taking lessons."

"No. She never wanted to drive. It was almost a phobia with her. I wanted her to come with me when I was taking lessons, but she just flat out refused. And she didn't have a car. I'm sure she would have said something about that – none of this makes any sense."

I can't quell the tears, or the sobs that some from nowhere and shake me to the core. She can't be gone. She just can't. Anton holds me close, until I get control of myself again. "Sorry," I say, stepping back and reaching into my pocket for a Kleenex. We look at each other blankly.

What do we do now? Maybe this is information we should share with the police. Or maybe it isn't. How can you prove someone didn't want to do something. There's no such thing as negative proof – or if there is, I've never heard of it. Would the police laugh at me if I told them something like that?

"What now?" I whisper.

"I don't know," Anton says.

Jeff makes a suggestion. "There should be a service of some kind, after they've finished the autopsy. Maybe we can find out where it will be – or who's going to be in charge of it." He pauses, then shakes his head. "No, I guess it's too early for any of that."

My mind clings to one word: autopsy. Images flash up: I know what an autopsy involves. I can't picture Sahira that way. I won't picture her like that - but the thoughts won't go away.

I take a deep breath. It doesn't help. "Jeff – where's the police station? I think we need to talk to someone there."

Jeff and Anton look at each other – a scary look that says they think I'm out of my mind. I guess I am. I haven't cried yet – but there are more important things to do, before I let myself break down.

"Okay. Do you want to follow me or go in my car?"

"I'll follow you."

"I'll go with you," Anton says.

What a rock he is. Always there when I need him. If he wasn't gay, I'd snap him up in a minute. I can't imagine a better life partner.

We retrieve my car and I follow Jeff to Battle Street. It isn't very far. We pull up in front of the red brick building, and walk in under the glass arch, trying to figure out where to go. "Traffic, maybe?" Jeff suggests.

"No – I think investigations." I ask at the information counter, and we're given directions to an office down the hall.

The constable we talk to is young. I wonder how experienced he is, or even if he'll believe me. "It's about the young woman who died in the motor vehicle accident – her car went off the road yesterday."

He nods. "What can I help you with?"

"I have a couple of questions – this is going to sound weird, but how did you identify her?"

He looks at me. Warily. I know I've said something wrong.

"I'm sorry, I can't give you that information."

"No – it's not what you think. She's my friend. She *was* my friend. My best friend." I bite my lips together and take a deep breath. I am not going to cry, I'm not gonna cry, I'mnotgonnacry...... I repeat it like a mantra, fighting for control.

"She used to be called Sahira, but she changed her name to Cassandra. She changed it legally, so she isn't Sahira Grewal any more, she's Cassandra Thompson now." He looks at me, wondering when I'm going to get to the point. "I mean, it's really strange that her identification says Sahira Grewal when that isn't her name any more ..." I run out of words. This is getting harder and harder.

"What's your relationship to her?"

"We used to live next door to each other. We grew up together, we went through school together – we've been like sisters, all our lives."

He's obviously weighing my words, balancing them against regulations. He comes to a decision, opens a drawer on the steel filing cabinet and pulls out a file. He flips it open, then looks up.

"She had ID in her purse – a driver's license with the name Sahira Kaur Grewal, and the car was registered in that name as well. I'm sorry, that's all I can tell you."

The file goes back into the drawer and it closes with a thump, like a metal exclamation point at the end of his statement.

I'm stunned. There is something wrong here. Very wrong. Not from his point of view – the license should be all that's required to identify her. But I know that it isn't right. I take a deep breath and hang on tight to the edge of the counter.

"That's not her license. Honest. She can't – she couldn't drive. She's never driven. And she didn't own a car. She's never owned a car."

He looks at me. It's a sympathetic look, but still full of authority. "According to these documents, she did."

I turn away, but Anton steps forward. "Can you tell us when the body will be released?"

"As soon as the family claims it."

"And if they don't?"

"Unless someone else ..." he comes to a full stop, looks at me, then turns back to Anton. "Look, are you sure you want to go into this now? Your friend is really upset."

"We're all upset. And yes, we need to know, because her family won't claim her."

"Why not?"

"Her father disowned her a year ago. He won't even admit she was ever his daughter."

There's a long silence. "I'm sorry to hear that. We still have to try to make contact with the family – but after that, if they're not willing and able to act, you can contact the Public Guardian and Trustee's office. You'll have some paper work to do. When that's finished, we have some personal effects here that the family might want."

"No. That won't happen either," Anton says.

The clock on the office wall beats out time, but it's slow. So slow. And loud. It's like everything is grinding to a halt, and the silence tightens around me. I have to say it. "When can we? I mean - where can we…" I can't finish, but Anton completes it for me.

"Where is she now?"

"At the hospital morgue – at the Royal Inland. She'll stay there until the Coroner has completed his investigation. I can't tell you how long it might take – it all depends on how quickly the test results are returned. Once that's done, she'll be taken to the funeral home. You can make arrangements with them and decide what kind of service you need, or whatever you want to do."

Jeff steps forward. "Okay, guys. I think that's all we need to know. Let's get out of here." He thanks the constable, and takes my arm. "Come on, Christie."

I stumble out of the building. It isn't fair. The sun is still shining. It shouldn't be shining when Sahira's dead.

"I gotta call my dad."

He answers quickly – almost like he's been waiting for my call.

"Dad – Sahira…"

"I know, honey. It was on the TV. Are you okay? Do you want me to come up there?"

I want. Yes, I want. I want my Dad's strong arms around me. I want him to tell me it's just a bad dream. I want him to wake me up. But that won't happen.

"No, I'm okay." And then suddenly, I'm not okay. All the tears I've held back explode in a tsunami of grief. I try to talk, but I can't make any words.

Anton takes the phone from my hand, and I hear him talking with my dad.

"Yes," he says. "We just came from the police station. They were very helpful. I don't think there will be any problems." There's more silence as he listens. "I understand. She's staying at the Days Inn – but I think it would be better if she came back to Jeff's place. We'll look after her until you get here."

Anton gives him Jeff's address and his phone number, then looks back at me. "Do you want to talk to your dad?"

I nod and take the phone. "Dad – I'm sorry. I just . . ."

He interrupts. "Look, just take it easy and stay with the guys. I'm on my way. Now let me talk to Anton again."

Before I hand the phone back, I whisper "I love you."

"I know that, kiddo. I'll be there as soon as I can get a flight."

When I hang up it feels like someone's cut my life line.

CHAPTER SEVENTEEN

I DON'T KNOW how Dad got here so fast, but I'm so glad to see him. Just to feel his arms around me and know he's going to look after things, makes me feel better. Inside, I rail at myself. *Way to go, Christie. That's being independent and grown-up.* I shut down the voice. I don't want to be independent. I don't want to be grown up. I want everything to go away and be like it used to. I want Sahira back.

Dad's voice rumbles in my ear.

"What? Sorry, I couldn't hear you."

He can't be saying what I thought he said. He repeats and it's as ugly as I thought it was.

"I went over to the Grewal house to talk to Sahira's dad. He wouldn't even look at me. All he said was 'I have no daughter.' Sorry – I wanted to get something from him that would let us claim…."

"Don't!" The sound is explosive, it bursts from me. "Don't. I know what you're going to say."

His arm tightens around me. "Okay. Take it easy. It's just that if her parents aren't going to claim her, I thought we could, and at least see she gets a proper service – so she isn't just abandoned."

Abandoned. There isn't an uglier word in the English language. Abandoned. Thrown away. Not worth anything to anybody. Dad's right. She doesn't deserve that, because she's worth lots. She's always been a warm, loving, intelligent person. She's been my closest friend for as long as I can remember. I can't imagine a future with no Sahira in it.

All she wanted was to be a veterinarian. Fix small, fuzzy animals. Make them well again. Give beloved pets back to their families. Make people happy.

I take a deep breath and look up at my dad. "It's okay. You're right. This is something we have to do – but I don't know how."

"I don't either," he admits. "But we can find out."

Jeff steps forward. Good old, reliable Jeff. "I can do that for you. When we went to the police station, they said we had to work through the Public Guardian and Trustee office. I don't know where that is, or what we have to do there, but I can find out."

Dad smiles. "That would be great. I think I'll take Christie out for a walk along the river – it's been a real shock for her. For all of us. I'm glad you and Anton were here to help her."

"I can get her car for you," Anton offers.

"Thanks. That would be great."

My car. I hadn't even thought about it. I hope it isn't covered with parking tickets or anything. I hand my keys to Anton. "Thanks." It's just a whisper, but it's all I can come up with right now.

Later that night, Jeff brings out some papers. "You'll have to get a court order, but you can do that back in Vancouver. They don't release – they won't ..." He stalls.

I interrupt. "How long until...?"

"Depends on the inquest results."

I take a deep breath and look at dad. He nods his head and says the words that I can't say.

"Maybe that's what we should do, then. Go back to Vancouver and do the paperwork there. We can send the documents up here and when it's time, we'll be here for her."

That's when the tears really start. Hot, horrid tears. I'm crying for me, I'm crying for Sahira, and I'm crying for all the dreams that will never come true. Dad grabs me, and holds me tight. He makes the little soothing noises that we've both made when Karli was upset. It hits me suddenly.

"Karli! Where's Karli?"

"It's okay," Dad says. "She's at the neighbours. They'll take good care of her."

"How long, I mean – when..." I'm not even thinking straight anymore.

"We can't do any more now," he says. "Come on Dorothy – click your heels together and let's head for home."

The drive home seems endless. Dad's driving my car, and Anton's sitting in the back seat. No one feels like talking. I guess we've each got some heavy thinking to do.

I can't believe how long this day has been. It's late when we get back to Vancouver. Anton gives me a quick hug when we drop him off at his place, then moments later, Dad pulls into our driveway. I open the car door and head for the house, but Dad's stalling around.

"What's wrong?" I ask.

"I'm just wondering if we should leave Karli next door or bring her home tonight. She's probably sound asleep by now," he says.

"She'll be happier tomorrow if she wakes up in her own bed."

Dad goes to retrieve her, while I open the front door, turn on the lights in the house and head up to her bedroom and make sure everything is in place. Minutes later, I hear them come in and Karli's calling my name.

"I'm up here," I call. "Just making sure your teddy bear is awake."

She giggles and scrambles up the stairs. I love this little girl with all my heart. We go through her bedtime routine, or what's left of it. She's already brushed her teeth and put on her pjs, but I brush her hair and help her wash her face.

"Tell me a story," she demands, as I tuck her into bed.

"Not tonight, pumpkin. It's really, really late. But we can read the comics in the morning."

She accepts that, and snuggles into her pillow as I tiptoe out of the room.

Then it's my turn. "Dad – I'm really, really tired. Would you mind if I just went to bed? We can talk in the morning."

"You're a mind-reader. I was thinking that too. It's been a long day – for both of us."

Dad and Karli are both up before me. I wake to the sound of her laughter, and the smell of Dad's coffee. He makes the best coffee in the world. Sorry, Starbucks, but it's true. It's a great way to wake up – but a few minutes later, memory rushes in and swamps my thoughts. Sahira. I'll never hear her laugh again. Never get a text from her. Never – *Stop it*, I command. *That's not doing any good.*

I head for the shower and a few minutes later, join Dad and Karli.

After breakfast, Dad's got a list of questions for me. The first is a little tricky.

"Sahira's family are Sikhs. I know that. But do you know which temple they belonged to?"

I laugh. "It isn't a temple, Dad. Sahira must have told me a thousand times not to call it a temple. It's a Gurdwara."

"Okay, but which one?"

"It's over in Surrey. I don't remember the name, but I know where it is."

"If we're going to have some kind of service for Sahira, that's where it should be. Right?"

Yeah. Right. Of course. But I don't even want to think about it now. It's like admitting she's really, truly gone.

He's still looking at me, waiting for an answer.

"Okay."

"Look, kiddo – I know this is hard, but this is something you can do for your friend. And I'd like to help you."

That starts the waterworks again. Jeez – when am I going to get through a day without turning into a blubbering idiot. And what's even worse, I'm upsetting Karli. Her little face is all crinkled up with concern.

"What's wrong, Christie?"

I take a deep breath and try to pull myself together. "It's okay, pumpkin." I give her a hug, then look at my dad. "Sorry. I didn't mean to fall apart like that."

"I think we should go and talk to the minister or whatever he's called, and find out what we can do for Sahira."

Dad's right. That's the logical thing to do, and the thing I really don't want to do. There's something so very wrong about this.

"Dad – would it help if I tried to talk to Sahira's dad? Ask him what he wants to do? Or her mom? They might have changed their minds. I mean, now that ..." *Hang on,* I tell myself. *You can do this. One step at a time. Okay. Try again.* "Now that Sahira's gone, the honour thing is – ended, or something? I don't know. But maybe I should try."

Dad looks like he's going to say something, then shakes his head. "That's a very kind thought – I'm really proud of you, Christie. Yeah – that would probably be the right thing to do. The police will have notified him by now. Maybe it was just shock that made him answer me the way he did." He swirls his spoon around in his coffee, watching the waves lap around in his cup. "Do you want me to come with you?"

"No – it will probably be easier if I go by myself. Maybe I can talk to her mom, if he doesn't want to talk to me."

After breakfast, I take the long journey to Sahira's house. The familiar steps are suddenly strange. I find myself walking slower and slower but eventually, her house is there. I walk into the front yard and up the steps. The same steps I've climbed hundreds of times before. My thumb automatically pushes the door bell. It's like I'm a robot, programmed to do all these things, but it isn't really me, doing them.

The door opens part way. Mr. Grewal fills the opening. He doesn't say anything, just looks at me.

"Mr. Grewal – I'm so sorry about what happened to Sah…" Her name isn't out of my mouth before the door closes. He doesn't say a word. My mind goes around in circles – what do I do now? Without thinking, my thumb presses the bell again and the door opens, a smaller crack this time.

"Please," I say. "I need to know what to do with her things, and about the funeral."

He looks at me. I have never seen such cold eyes in my life. They are colder than the glistening eyes of a snake. And they are dead. There is no hatred, there is no emotion of any kind. Just glittering dark eyes, staring deep into mine. It's almost a physical thing and it's all I can do not to jump back.

"I have no daughter."

The door closes. Not with a bang. Not slammed. It simply shuts. I lean against it, too wrung out to cry. After a minute, I turn and walk away.

At home, Dad hugs me tightly, rocking me in his arms. "Go ahead," he whispers. "Let it all out."

"Sorry. Sorry to be such a baby. I didn't think he would be like that."

"Well, now we know. Do you still want to do this?"

"Yeah. I do. Jeff says it's usually about 60 days until we …." I bite my lips together. Hard, and take a deep breath. "To pick up the ashes."

"Okay. We can work from there. I'll contact TRU and have them clear out her room – unless you want to do it?"

I shake my head. "I'm not sure what's going to happen there – they probably don't even know that she's… that she's not there any more. The ID was for Sahira Grewal but they know her as Sandy Thompson." A deep breath escapes from far inside me. Why does everything have to be so complicated? "We'll probably have to do more paperwork." I pause, thinking about Sahira's possessions. "There probably isn't much anyway – she didn't have anything. Just her books and a few clothes."

"Okay. We can look after that. Now about the temple – sorry – what did you call it?"

"The Gurdwara."

"Okay. Should we go to the one where her dad goes? Or would you rather pick another one?"

I start to laugh. There's no way I'm going to let that miserable old man deny Sahira her funeral, and I really don't think he deserves to be there. Then I realize he's solved the problem already. "The family used to go to one in Surrey – that's where they know her best. But he doesn't go there any more. When the new Port Mann Bridge opened, he got all upset about having to pay tolls, so he started going to the one up in Mission." I stop for a minute, gathering my thoughts. "Yes, I think we should go to the one in Surrey because that's the one Sahira liked best."

"Okay. We'll talk to the minister or whatever he's called, and find out what to do next."

I feel so helpless. And mad at myself. It's frustrating that I know so little about some parts of Sahira's life. I know she and her mom served in the Langar, the Gurdwara kitchen, giving out free food to those in need and to other members of the community, but there's so much I don't know about her beliefs, what was important to her, and what really mattered in the end.

When Dad and I get to the Gurdwara, I try to visualize it though Dad's eyes. I'd gone a couple of times, years and years ago, when Sahira and I were both just little kids. I'd almost forgotten what it was like. Now I look at it with new eyes – seeing it the way Dad must be seeing it ... just a large, empty room, with carpet on the floor. No seats and no benches.

"Where do they sit?" Dad whispers.

"On the floor," I say. "There's a lot of getting up and kneeling down. Well, sort of kneeling. I guess it's prostrating themselves. At least, that's what the men do. The women sit upstairs in the balcony. They don't do all the kneeling and stuff."

We ask some of the people inside where the man in charge is and they direct us to him. Dad asks for the minister, and they're very polite about correcting him: he's not a minister, he's the Granthis. I guess it's the same thing. Well, probably not, but he's sort of their leader. Luckily, there are chairs in his office and we don't have to sit on the floor. Dad does most of the talking.

"This is going to sound pretty weird," he begins, "and we don't really know what we're asking – but a friend of ours has died and we'd like to have some sort of service for her – a service of remembrance."

I can tell Dad wants to give a better explanation, but he doesn't really know how. "I guess that sounds pretty bizarre," he adds.

Granthis wig-wags his hand, cutting Dad off. "Nothing is bizarre. Things may surprise us, but they are what they are meant to be. Karma controls our lives."

It takes a minute to get past that, then Dad begins again.

"Our friend belonged to your church." He corrects himself quickly. "Your Gurdwara. We want to make sure she has a proper memorial service. And pay for her headstone."

The Granthis smiles then – a very sweet, soft smile. Not a flat-out happy-face smile, not a laughing-at-us-smile, but a recognition of kindness.

"We don't have graves and headstones. A body is just a shell. The soul is the real essence of a person. Your friend's soul has returned to its starting point. We can only guess what her next step will be."

There's a pause, then the Granthis asks a question.

"What was your friend's name?"

I chime in. "Sahira. Sahira Grewal."

He nods. "Ah, yes. I remember the family." He thinks for a moment. "I believe they went to Mission – why wouldn't you have the service there?"

Dad takes over. "This isn't a happy story – but she disobeyed her father, and he disowned her. He won't even acknowledge that he has a daughter... had a daughter. There aren't any other relatives here." Dad looks at me. "Sahira and my daughter have been friends for a long time. She's pretty much been part of our family all her life - and we'd like to do whatever is right for her now." He stops, like he's trying to decide what to say next. "Your temple - sorry, your Gurdwara - is the one that meant the most to Sahira. I'm not sure that she even went to the one in Mission - I think that happened after she'd left home."

There's another silence that seems to last forever, while the Granthis weighs what my dad has told him, and thinks about the options.

"It is complicated, isn't it," he begins. "I'm sorry for your loss - and sorry for her family as well. Usually, when a family member dies, we have a service that begins with a complete reading of the Guru Granth Sahib - our holy book. That takes about ten days. Most families like to do that themselves - take turns with the reading so everyone has the opportunity to take part. The end of the reading marks the beginning of a new cycle - for the family and for the one who has left them." He looks at us carefully. He already knows we aren't going to do the reading - or rather, that we can't do it. He nods to himself before continuing. "If there is no family to read for her, there are people in the Gurdwara who will do that. It will be a blessing."

I'm not sure if it's a blessing for them or for her, but I don't want to interrupt.

"Most often," he continues, "the body is cremated and the ashes are scattered in water - running water, or open ocean."

I turn to dad. "She was happy at TRU. Maybe it would be good to ..." it's hard to say the words, but the Granthis smiles and nods, as though he's encouraging me. "We could put her ashes in the river, near the university."

There's a bit more as Dad and the Granthis settle some details, but I dial out and think about Sahira. I remember one time she came home from a party with henna tattoos on her hands.

"Look what I've got," she said, stretching her hands out for me to see.

"What's that?"

"It's part of the Mehandi - something brides do before they get married."

I've never heard the word before, so she explains. "It's a henna ceremony. Well, it's called a ceremony but it's more like a party for the bride and her girlfriends. I guess it's almost the equivalent of a shower the women in your church have before they get married. For us, the bride gets tattooed a couple of days before the wedding. Her hands, feet, sometimes her back and her neck. Her friends get tattooed too, but it's usually just their hands. Look - see how pretty it is? There are special artists who do this - it takes a long time, but it's very beautiful."

It is pretty, but ... "I'm not sure I'd want to have that on my hands forever," I say.

She laughs. "It isn't really a tattoo – the henna wears off in a couple of weeks, but it is lovely, isn't it?"

Now she'll never have those beautiful tattoos before her wedding day. Never graduate from TRU, never become a vet. Never do any of the things that should have filled her future. I suddenly realize both men are looking at me.

"Christie, are you ready to go?" Dad nudges me. He grabs my hand and squeezes it as we get to our feet.

"Yes." I turn to the Granthis. "Thank you. Thank you very much. This means a lot to me – and I think it's important to Sahira too."

He places his hands together and brings them up in front of his face, like praying hands. I think he's going to say something icky, but he doesn't. He bends his head over his hands briefly, and somehow, I understand. He's telling me not to grieve for Sahira – that she's at peace now. At least, that's what it feels like he's saying.

Over the next few days, I try not to think about it, but other times, me and Anton talk about what happened, trying to figure out where things went so wrong.

"The more I think about it, the more I'm convinced that it was an honour killing," I tell him. "There are just too many things that don't fit. Like the driver's license. And the car – my god – Sahira buying a car? No way. She was saving up to get her vet's training in Saskatchewan. She didn't have that kind of money. And even if she did, she'd never use it for that."

"So who do you think is responsible?" Anton asks. "Her dad?"

"Probably," I agree. "I don't think he actually did it – but he probably got someone to do it for him."

"But her mom –"

I cut him off. "Her mom wouldn't have any say in it. He ran that household. Ran it like an army camp. Sahira and her mom did what they were told. And they didn't argue. I'd bet on it." I remembered the few times Sahira had been unhappy about something her dad did, or said, or insisted that she had to do, whether she wanted to or not. There was never any argument. She just did as she was told. And I would have bet anything that her mom was just the same.

"I know it wasn't an accident," I repeat, "but I don't know how to prove it."

Life rumbles along. Funny how that happens. I'm starting to getting used to the idea that Sahira is gone. I never thought that could happen. Now we're just waiting until all the paper work is cleared. Dad promised we could go to pick up Sahira's ashes, the Granthis notified the congregation, and the special reading got underway. We wrote to TRU to let them know what happened. They put her stuff in storage and said they'd keep it until someone claimed it. They'll rent her room out to someone else – there's always a waiting list. It's as though the ripple of her life has gotten smaller and smaller, and is almost played out.

Too soon, or at last, I don't know how to think about it any more, the funeral home notifies us that all the paperwork is completed and we are authorized to pick up her ashes.

"Are you sure you want to do this?" Dad asks.

"Yeah. I'm sure."

"Okay. We'll go up on Friday. That gives us the weekend to look after everything."

He gives me a hug. There's something so special in a Dad-hug. It's like building a protective wall around you. Nothing bad can get in.

"Thanks, Dad." Then I think of something else. "Do you think Anton would like to come with us? I was going to scatter her ashes in the river, near the university. It's moving water, like the Granthis said – and it's one place that I know she was happy."

"Good idea. While we're there, we can pick up the stuff from the police station too."

I'd almost forgotten about that. Her purse was in the car, and it's still being held at the station.

Friday comes and we head up country. Karli's a ray of sunshine. She's excited about everything she sees. We play word games in the car, make up silly rhymes, and make lots of stops on the way. I love that little girl more and more. It's mid-afternoon when we arrive in Kamloops.

"Look, I know you've got stuff to do," Anton says. "Why don't I take Karli for the afternoon. We can get something to eat," he turns to her. "Would you like that Karli?" Her grin has McDonald's written all over it, but Anton isn't finished yet. "And then maybe we can find a playground."

Karli beams. "With a round and round?"

"If we're lucky. I'm sure we can find lots to do." He turns to me, "We'll meet you back at Jeff's place."

What a great guy. He's so damned thoughtful – it almost makes me cry. But I'm not going to give way to more tears. I'm all cried out. I give Karli a hug. "You look after Anton, okay?" She's happy calling him Anton now, instead of William, and never even asks why his name has changed. Little kids are so great – they just accept things and carry on with their lives.

We pick up Sahira's ashes, then head on to the police station to gather the rest of her stuff.

The same constable is on duty when we go in. I'm amazed, but he remembers us. We show our paperwork and he brings out a cardboard box. Nothing fancy – just a plain old box – and digs out Sahira's purse.

"This is all that was in the car," he says, handing it over. "Can you check the contents, please, and then initial the receipt?"

I open the purse and take out her wallet. For some reason, I flip it open. Her driver's license stares back at me. The eyes in the black and white photo are blank and empty. Not like Sahira's eyes at all. Not like … I gasp.

"Dad – this isn't Sahira!"

"What?" He grabs the wallet from me and pulls the license out of its slot. He looks closely. "No, it isn't." He holds it out to the constable. "This isn't Sahira. It looks a lot like her – but it isn't her."

Now it's the constable's turn to be shocked. "Are you sure?"

"Absolutely," Dad says.

"It really isn't," I add. "I knew there was something wrong when we were here before and you said she had a driver's license."

The constable leans on the counter and takes the license back as I rummage in the box. There's an envelope in the bottom. I open it – the vehicle registration papers. I spread them on the counter and look at them.

"These were issued in Vancouver," I say, pointing to the document. "But she wasn't there then. She was up here. At school. And look at this." I point to her signature, "This isn't her signature. That's the address where her parents live, and that's her birthday. But …."

Dad sums it up. "These are fakes. No – not fakes. They're frauds. Someone's gone to a lot of trouble to create an identity. But it isn't real."

The constable straightens up. "That's a serious allegation."

Dad looks at him. "I know. But trust me – there's something very wrong about this whole affair."

The constable opens the file folder again. "The coroner's report shows a skull fracture and that she broke her neck – that's consistent with what might happen when a car rolls over and the driver isn't wearing a seat belt, so there wasn't any suspicion of foul play."

"Maybe," I say, "But those documents are forgeries. Or fakes. They aren't hers at all. And if they're fake, then it's got to be a cover-up for something. And that means that what happened was no accident."

The constable looks from me to dad, then comes to some decision. "I'll have to take a statement," he says, "And we'll have to hold on to these as evidence."

I put the wallet back in the purse, along with the registration papers, and hand it back to him. He puts it back in the cardboard box, and returns it to the drawer.

"What happens now?" I ask.

"Now we try to find out what's going on. Who's done this – and why," he says.

I know why. Dad and I look at each other. Should I tell him what I think? I take a deep breath, and face the constable.

"Look – this is going to sound melodramatic, but there's something you should know. Sahira's parents had arranged a marriage for her. She was supposed to go to India, to marry this guy she'd never met. Someone the same age as her father. She didn't want to do it, so she ran away and I came with her. That was almost a year ago. She had a scholarship to the university, and I worked planting trees.

"I know it looks like a car accident, but I think it was an honour killing. That's why the false ID and everything. It was all a massive coverup, which means this whole thing was planned out.

"I've known Sahira all my life. She couldn't drive – she never even wanted to learn. She didn't have a car. She was living on her scholarship and a few dollars she got working in the library, stacking books. Even if she could have afforded a car, she wouldn't have used her money for that. After she graduated from TRU, she was supposed to go to Saskatchewan, to complete her veterinarian's training. And she was saving every penny she could to pay for that, because she had to pay for it herself. Like my dad told you before, her parents disowned her, so they weren't about to help her. In any way, shape or form."

The constable rubs his forehead. "Wow. That's quite a story."

"You can confirm it pretty easily," Dad says. "Grewal won't even acknowledge that he has a daughter. We tried to visit him after she died, but he just shut the door in our face and tells us he doesn't have a daughter. But he did. And that was Sahira."

"I don't know whose picture is on the license is, but it isn't Sahira. Don't take my word for it - you can check with the university. They'll tell you she was in class during the day, and working her shift in the library after classes ended, on the day that driver's license was issued. So there's no way she could be in Vancouver taking a driving test."

Now the constable is all business. "Okay. Let's get an official statement here."

It's like living in a movie script. This can't be happening, but it is. He asks a lot of questions, writing down all our answers. The questions seem to go on forever, but eventually he looks up and smiles.

"Thank you. You did a good thing, bringing this to our attention. And I know how hard it must have been for you." He pulls out another form. "Where can we contact you?"

I give him Dad's address and he writes it down. Then we're free to go, but there's question I have to ask. It's been bothering me for months now.

"Is there anything I should have done – something that might have …. could have…."

The constable shakes his head. "No. There's nothing you could have done, so don't feel guilty – it's hard to help people when they won't ask for help. We run into this all the time – women who have obviously been beaten, but who won't press charges. You might have been able to convince your friend to ask for help, or you might not." He reaches into a drawer and pulls out a small card. "This is the Tri-City Transitions number – they offer help, counselling, alternate housing or temporary shelter. It might have helped your friend. There's actually a Canada-wide network at ShelterNet.ca, that gives addresses for assistance in any city in Canada." He hands me the card. "Just for future reference." He looks at my dad and smiles. "I don't imagine you'll need it, but if you ever meet someone who is in a difficult situation, this is a good starting point."

We leave the building and stand outside the police station for a minute. The sun feels warm.

"What now?" Dad asks.

"I think we should scatter her ashes – like we planned to do."

He grabs my hand. "You know, sometimes you remind me so much of your mother. You're the same wonderful mix of strength and kindness that she was."

And then I do choke up. I take a deep breath and look at him. It takes a minute before I can get my voice under control. "Okay, Dad. I can't stand here blubbering for the whole world to see. Come on – let's just do it."

Dad drives to a little park, along the river's edge, and hands me the container. I open it slowly, then tip it into the water, and as the ashes trickle out I whisper to her. "I'm so sorry, Sahira. I never imagined this would happen. But he won't get away with it. I promise you."

When the container is empty, I throw it into the water too.

"Okay. Let's go get Karli."

CHAPTER EIGHTEEN

I'D EXPECTED A long wait, but things move along pretty fast. The day after we get home, a police car pulls up to the door and two constables come up the walk. There's something about the way policemen walk – even if they weren't in uniform, you could tell who they were. After introducing themselves, the older officer pulls out a sheaf of notes.

"I understand you were a friend of Sahira Grewal?"

"Yes, I was."

"According to our report, you think the ID in her purse was fraudulent?"

I nod. "I know it was."

"Okay. What makes you think so?"

"Because the picture on her driver's license isn't her. And the signature isn't hers."

"Do you have anything to corroborate that?"

"Sure do," I say. I get out our high school yearbook and flip to Sahira's grad picture. "This is her. The girl in that picture looks something like her – maybe close enough if you didn't really look at it, or if you didn't know her. But it isn't Sahira." I flip to the back of the book where all the autographs were. "And here – here's her signature. It's not even close to the one on the registration form."

He reaches for the book. "We'll need that for evidence."

I'm reluctant to hand it over. "Will I get it back?"

He smiles. "Yes. I'll make sure you do." He holds the yearbook in his hands, balanced on his palms, like he's weighing it – weighing evidence or something. "Any idea why someone would do this?"

I think about what I'm going to say, debating whether I should tell him my suspicions or not. I guess the constable in Kamloops didn't write down anything about an honour killing. I don't want to sound stupid, but... There isn't a 'but'. Nothing is more important than finding out who did this. If I'm wrong, then I'm wrong. But if I'm right, I owe it to Sahira to speak up.

"This might sound a crazy, but I think it was an honour killing, made to look like an accident. There's just too many things that are wrong. Sahira never drove – never wanted to learn. She freaked out at the idea of driving. And she didn't have a car. The license and the car registration were issued down here. But I looked at the dates when they were issued, and Sahira wasn't here – she was in Kamloops on those dates. She was a student at Thompson River University – they'll have records, so you can check that out."

The constables look at each other, then the older one speaks. "An honour killing? What did she do that might have prompted that?"

"Her dad had arranged for her to marry some guy in the Punjab. Someone she'd never met – who was the same age as her dad. Some kind of cousin. She was okay right up until it was time to leave for India – and that's when she realized what she was getting into. And..." I have to compose myself. I'm not going to cry. I'm *not*. I begin again. "When it came right down to it, she couldn't do it, so she ran away. I helped her. We both went up to Kamloops. Her dad was furious – so mad that he won't even admit that he had a daughter. He disowned her completely. And that's what makes me think it was an honour killing." I look at him. He's not laughing – he's listening and taking it seriously. "And – there was no reason for anyone else to do this. She didn't have any enemies."

The first constable nods as I'm speaking. "Okay. We tried to talk to the dad, but he refused to discuss his daughter."

The second constable hasn't said a word so far, but he's been taking notes while we talk. "Did you talk to Sahira's mom?" I ask. The first guy shakes his head. "No. We'll do that later." He looks at the other constable. "I guess we're done here."

They leave, taking my yearbook with them. I feel empty inside, like I've sent them off on a fruitless quest. Like I know they aren't going to find out anything by talking to Sahira's mom.

When dad comes home, I tell him about the interview.

"I don't know if they believed me or not – but if you looked at the picture in the yearbook, you could see it wasn't Sahira on the driver's license."

"Well, maybe they can find out who got the license. That would be a lead," he says. "But whoever planned this probably didn't leave very many clues lying around."

"This is where I think I should be writing murder mysteries," I say. "Being smart enough to find that one little clue that will to solve everything."

Dad laughs. "I've always been suspicious about those 'aha!' moments in a mystery story. I sometimes think they dream up the clues first, and then write the story around them."

"Maybe they do."

Then dad has another question. "Did they say anything about the autopsy report?"

I shake my head. "Nope. Not a word, and I never thought to ask them." I think about it for a minute. "I don't know if they'd tell me about it in any case. I mean, as far as they're concerned, we're probably not entitled to that kind of information."

Dad's question starts me thinking. If they did toxicology tests, that would tell if she'd been drugged or anything. Maybe she was unconscious before someone put her in the car. I hoped so. But even that wouldn't be enough – they had to have killed her – hit her on the head or something. Her neck could have snapped when the car rolled down the hill. The newspaper said she was on a learner's license. I know that means she was supposed to have someone else in the car with her – someone who had a regular license. But she was the only one in the car. And the story said she wasn't wearing a seat belt.

Sahira would never have gotten into a car without doing up her seat belt. Never. She went fucking overboard about following rules. Drove me up the wall at times, but that was just the way she was. So as far as I'm concerned, that's just another thing that points to this being something other than an accident. I know they can't do toxicology now, because she's already been cremated, and there was no reason to do it before, because it looked like a simple accident. But maybe they kept tissue samples, and they could still determine whether she'd been drugged or not? Maybe, maybe, maybe. There are just so many loose ends. I guess the bottom line is, I've been reading too many murder mysteries and watching who-dunnits on TV.

"Well," dad says, "There's nothing more we can do right now."

He's right, but it's easier to say you should get on with your life, than to do it. I'm back to my writing classes, but every time I try to write something, I start thinking about Sahira. I know dad was joking, but maybe if I tried to write a mystery story based on the whole rotten mess, I might be able to find that missing link.

The police photocopied Sahira's picture in the yearbook, and her signature in the back of the book, then returned it to me.

"My daughter graduated a couple of years ago," the constable said, when he handed it back. "I know how much it meant to her, and I know yours is even more precious – because of your friend."

"Thank you," I said. He had no idea how glad I was to have it back.

Since then, we haven't heard anything. Dad and I talk, once in a while, probing at that unsolved mystery. There has to be something – some little thing that we haven't noticed – that could unravel this whole mess. But I can't think of what it might be. Or where we should look.

"Do you think they'll ever find out who did it?" I ask.

"We may never know who actually did it," dad says, "but there's not much doubt in my mind, about who is responsible. That's the thing, though. He might be responsible, but it's pretty hard to pin anything on him. I mean, it's going to be really hard even to prove responsibility if they don't catch the guy who actually did it. And unfortunately, the one who is responsible could only be charged as an accessory."

"Even her injuries aren't conclusive," Dad says, "but I can't see someone just putting her in the car, and pushing the car over the cliff. People have survived some pretty horrendous crashes. And in any case, she would have struggled."

"Unless she'd been hit on the head or something. I mean, if she was unconscious, it would be easy to do."

Dad agrees with me. "That's probably what happened. We'll never know if she was drugged so she couldn't put up a struggle, or if something else happened."

"I have to believe they gave her something and she passed out before anything happened," I say. "That way she wouldn't even know that she was going over the bank, and she wouldn't suffer."

Neither of us is willing to say what we fear – that Sahira's neck was broken before she was placed in the car, then the car was pushed over the embankment.

Meanwhile, Dad went back to the Gurdwara and had several talks with the Granthis. Funnily enough, his name is Gurbash – the same name as the guy Sahira was supposed to marry. It's got to be just a coincidence, but dad related some of the things Gurbash told him – about the Sikh belief that everything happens for a reason, and that your future is known to God. It almost seemed like if Sahira didn't choose the path that had one Gurbash in it, she would have to choose another – and it would have a Gurbash in it too. It sort of fit in with the 'circle of life' that dad and the Granthis talked about.

More importantly, we decided that since there wasn't going to be any burial or headstone or anything, we wanted the Granthis to help set up a small bursary for a university entrance student. It would go to a girl, preferably from his congregation and, of Punjabi ancestry. I went with dad to their final meeting.

"A very nice memorial," the Granthis said, after all the documents had been signed. "Who will present it to the young woman who wins it? One of you?" He looked at me, then at dad.

Dad thought a bit about that. I could almost hear his mind turning over, and then we both smiled. He turned back to the Granthis and said, "No, I don't think so. We'll just call it the Sahira Grewal Memorial Scholarship, from an anonymous donor."

The Granthis smiled. It was almost like he knew that's what we'd say. "That is very fitting and very generous."

Life went on pretty uneventfully after that. The days drifted by, one after another and we all got back to our usual routines - that is, until the morning I tried to teach Karli how to tie up her shoelaces. Up till now, all her shoes have had Velcro-strap closures, but her new sneakers have laces. I show her how to do it, and she tries and tries, but her fingers just can't make the bow properly. That's when she rips the shoe from her foot and slams it against the floor. "Shit."

Dad bends down and ties the laces for her, then walks her to the school, like he always does. When he gets back, he calls me into the kitchen and gestures toward a chair. I know what's coming.

"I guess we both heard what Karli said," he begins, but I interrupt. "I know. I'm sorry – I guess she heard me say it."

"It seems to be something you say quite often. That and a few other choice phrases." He looks at me. "What do you think we should do about it?"

A dozen things run through my head – I'd heard about kids getting their mouths washed out with soap when they used bad language. Or being sent to their room. Or any number of other punishments. I start to say something, but Dad cuts me off.

"I'm not going to punish her, because it's not her fault."

The words hang there, waiting for comment. I take a deep breath. "I'll try to be more careful," I promise.

"Do that."

He changes the subject, and nothing more is said about it. But I really, really tried hard to use better language when I was around Karli. And a couple of times, when she said something that I knew Dad didn't want to hear, I'd give her another word to use. The next time she said 'shit' I told her that big girls liked to use bigger words than that.

"You don't," she replied.

"No," I laughed. "Sometimes I don't, but that's just because I get lazy. You can help me remember. There's lots of other words we can use."

"Like what?"

"Oh, like ...." From somewhere, a word floated to the surface of my mind. "How about 'platypus'?"

Her expression was pure disdain. I wasn't fooling her one little bit. "Nope. That' not a real word."

"Well, yeah, it is. It's a kind of little animal."

"That's just silly. You don't say 'dog' or 'cat', so why should I say pol, pla, whatever it was you said?"

"Okay, how about just saying 'poly.' 'Oh, poly' sounds a lot better than 'oh, shit.' And anyways, you'll get in trouble in school if you say that, but the teacher won't care if you say 'oh, poly'." She tried the word out, pursing her lips together like she was tasting it, then spitting out 'poly', only it came out 'plappy' instead, with a loud, percussive 'p' at the beginning, almost verging on 'pappy'.

"Yeah. I like that. But you have to say it too."

I did, and Dad did his best not to laugh the first time he heard me say it.

One thing about Karli – you never know what she's going to come up with. She has more imagination than any other kid I know, but she outdid herself one morning just before the start of the Christmas holidays.

She was now in her first year at school – 'real school' she calls it. She loves it – but for some reason, there's a hassle almost every morning, trying to get her to finish her breakfast in time to leave for school. She is the slowest eater I've ever seen.

That particular morning, I couldn't believe what I was seeing.

"Karli, why are you eating your Cheerios one at a time?"

She looks at me with that lovely little smile, then picks another Cheerio out of the bowl and pops it in her mouth. "I learned a new word at school yesterday, and this is what it does."

Dad rolls his eyes. "And what was the word?"

"Nibble," she says. "Nibble like a bunny rabbit does. So I'm being a bunny rabbit, and I'm learning how to nibble."

Dad chokes as he tries to stifle a laugh, and finally gets himself under control. "Karli, I don't think your teacher meant for you to be late for school. Sometimes even bunny rabbits have to eat quickly – so I suggest you pretend you've just seen a big dog jump over the fence and run towards you. What do you think that bunny rabbit would do then?"

"He'd run away, just as fast as he can," she laughed.

"Right," Dad says. "So now it's time for you to make like a bunny rabbit get ready as fast as you can because unless you do, you're going to be late for school."

She looks at the rest of her Cheerios, then at dad and says "Okay." In one big motion she scoops a huge spoonful of Cheerios into her mouth, slides down from her chair and heads for the front hall. She squirms into her coat before dad can even get up from the table.

He puts down the paper he's been reading and follows her, grabbing his jacket as they head out the door. He walks her to school every morning. It's sort of sweet. I wish he'd walked me to school when I was little, but that's when we were struggling through my first step-mother and then a series of girlfriends. Things were pretty different then. I'm glad, for Karli's sake, that things aren't like that now.

After they leave, I pick up the paper and thumb through it. I don't usually bother reading it – most of it just repeats what was on the TV last night. But today, an item on one of the inside pages catches my eye.

FREAK ACCIDENT NEAR WHISTLER

A Vancouver couple died yesterday in a freak accident near Whistler Village, when a logging truck overturned and lost its load, spilling logs onto an oncoming car. The deceased, identified as Parmar and Gurjeet Grewal, were the sole occupants of the vehicle. The driver of the truck sustained minor injuries. Police have not released further details.

This is the fourth incident involving logging trucks losing their loads along the Sea to Sky highway. Earlier incidents involved a fatality when a motorcyclist was crushed by falling logs, and two other incidents involving crushed passenger vehicles resulting in severe injuries, but no deaths.

A member of the local Concerned Citizens group said Whistler residents are outraged at the series of accidents, and insist that regulations regarding logging trucks need to be reviewed.

"Those trucks are either overloaded, the loads are fastened insecurely, or they are speeding. In any case, new regulations are needed and enforcement of those regulations has to happen immediately."

I can't believe what I'm reading. I look again. Those are the names of Sahira's parents. My mind slips back to the last interview Dad and I had with the Granthis.

"Karma," he said "Always. Karma decides our final outcome."

Karma. The circle of life.

For the first time since Sahira's death, my mind relaxes. Suddenly, it doesn't matter about the inquest, or the investigation. That will all be resolved eventually. The police may or may not ever find out what actually happened, or who actually did it. But that no longer seems important. It feels like justice has been done. Justice or Karma, or whatever you want to call it. In that moment, I realize what it is I'm supposed to do: I'll write my book and it will be Sahira's story. That will be my way of remembering her.

Dad's enthusiastic about it – but he's full of advice (as always). "You're going to have to do some research," he tells me. "I has to be accurate or no one is going to read it. Or believe it."

"I've done a little research already," I tell him. I have and it's absolutely terrifying. The AHA Foundation, in New York, supports women's rights and they have all sorts of facts and figures. When I first read it, I found it hard to believe their estimate that 5,000 women are victims of honour attacks every year. That's a world-wide estimate, and it includes women in North America. In a two-year period, they believe almost 3,000 women in North America have been victimized. Some women are killed outright, some grievously injured. Some are splashed with acid – blinded, or scarred for life. The experts say there are probably many more, because often they are made to look like accidents – to protect the families of the women, and the perpetrators.

They aren't all honour killings - many are killed or injured every year in domestic 'accidents' – another word for domestic violence. Too many women are afraid to report these events, which are usually referred to as 'domestic incidents'. I have to laugh at that word. Incidents. According to my dictionary, an incident is a 'subordinate or accessory event' - something small, not worth very much or not something anyone pays a great deal of attention to. Something that is life-threatening is hardly an incident but too many women choose to stay silent, and too many families hide the facts. Perhaps because they don't have the support they need to take a stand. Or maybe because they think no one will believe them if they do speak out.

Nothing will change, unless it becomes an issue – a huge, public issue. That's when I realize what I hope my book will do: create outrage. Make people who read, mad. Really mad. Mad enough to take a hard look at all those 'accidents' and start bringing the perpetrators to justice. Mad enough to start reporting injuries, and suspicious events. Mad enough to take a stand and ensure that women can report violence and be believed.

Somehow I have to begin Sahira's story. It's going to hurt and I know I'll cry while I'm writing it, but it's the only thing I can do for the lovely girl who was once my very best friend.

CPSIA information can be obtained
at www.ICGtesting.com
Printed in the USA
LVHW090505060320
649199LV00001B/57